SCARED!

"Holly, leave her alone," Liz said quickly, and then she put her hand reassuringly on Kerry's arm. "It's okay, Kerry. Don't be afraid to admit that you don't like horses. Not everyone's a horse-crazy maniac like Holly and me."

"I do like horses," Kerry admitted carefully. "But . . . but I'm scared of them." She hoped her lie was convincing enough to fool Holly and her mother.

"I'm so glad you're going to work here," Holly said with enthusiasm. "I think we could have a lot of fun together, don't you, Kerry?"

Yes, Kerry thought to herself as she looked at Holly's cheerful smile. But only if she didn't have to go to the stables. She just wasn't ready for that.

BEST FRIENDS

NO TIME
FOR SECRETS

BY MAGGIE DANA

ILLUSTRATIONS BY DONNA RUFF

Troll Associates

To Melanie, Paul, and Peter

Library of Congress Cataloging in Publication Data

Dana, Maggie.
    No time for secrets.

    (Best Friends; #1)
    Summary: When thirteen-year-old Kerry takes a job as
companion to a handicapped girl whose mother runs a
stables, she knows she eventually will have to deal
with a past incident that has made her want to stay
away from the horses she once loved.
    [1. Horses—Fiction.   2. Physically handicapped—
Fiction. 3. Friendship—Fiction] I. Ruff, Donna, ill.
II. Title.   III. Series: Best friends (Mahwah, N.J.); #1.
PZ7.D194No   1988   [Fic]   87-19027
ISBN 0-8167-1191-7 (lib. bdg.)
ISBN 0-8167-1192-5 (pbk.)

A TROLL BOOK, published by Troll Associates,
Mahwah, NJ 07430

Printed in the United States of America.

10 9 8 7 6 5 4 3 2 1

Chapter One

Kerry Logan rode down the tree-shaded road, deep in thought, paying no attention at all to her surroundings. With her head bent down over the handlebars, she ignored the early summer beauty that was all around her. Shafts of sunlight streamed down through the trees, highlighting the auburn streaks in her thick, wavy brown hair that now curled damply around her face. And, as Kerry nervously wiped the sweat off her forehead, her wide-set green eyes betrayed the conflicting emotions that were churning around inside her.

This is it, she thought to herself as she rounded the last corner on her aunt's ancient ten-speed. Ahead of her was a rambling old house, its weather-beaten siding showing signs of age. The lawn was liberally sprinkled with bright yellow dandelions and looked as if it hadn't been mowed in weeks. Beyond the house, Timber Ridge Mountain dominated the sky-

1

line, its now green ski trails spilling down its sides like dribbles of paint.

Kerry skidded the bicycle to a stop, sending a small shower of gravel out behind her. She winced, hoping she wasn't tearing the threadbare tires to pieces. Aunt Molly wouldn't be too thrilled if she came back with a puncture.

For a moment she hesitated, wondering if she was doing the right thing. It had seemed like a good idea that morning when she showed the Help Wanted ad to Aunt Molly. Kerry leaned against the bicycle and fumbled around in her pocket. She carefully withdrew the crumpled newspaper clipping and read the familiar words once again.

Mature young woman needed as companion to handicapped fourteen-year-old. Must be cheerful and hardworking. Would prefer someone who can live in. Call Timber Ridge Stables at 555-5739.

As Kerry read the words, she couldn't help smiling. The Help Wanted ad had almost sent Aunt Molly into a tailspin! She really loved her aunt, but sometimes she was too overprotective. Molly Russell had never had any kids of her own, and she didn't seem to understand that Kerry was going crazy from boredom. A whole summer, maybe even longer, stuck in Winchester, Vermont, with nothing to do.

Kerry wished that her father hadn't taken his latest job assignment, or that she could have gone with him. At least that would have helped to take her mind off what had happened just before she left Connecticut. Ben Logan, Kerry's father, was an engineer with a large oil company, and he'd been sent to the Middle East, to what was considered a high-risk area. There was no way a thirteen-year-old girl could accompany him. So Kerry had been sent up to Vermont to stay with her aunt.

"But why a job?" Aunt Molly had protested when Kerry showed her the advertisement.

"Because I'll go crazy if I don't have something to do," Kerry had replied. "I don't know anyone here, none of your friends have kids my age, and if I read one more book, I think I'll scream!"

"You could always go riding," Aunt Molly had answered.

Kerry shook her head sadly and stuffed the newspaper clipping back in her pocket, thinking about what Aunt Molly had innocently suggested. She had no way of knowing that Kerry had put horses—and riding—firmly out of her life.

And yet, here she was, applying for a job at Timber Ridge Stables. It didn't make much sense, but with a bit of luck, the job wouldn't involve horses. If it did, she just wouldn't take it. After what had happened, she didn't know if she was ready to face another horse. The whole thing had been a freak accident, but deep down, Kerry blamed herself. A horse, a beautiful horse that she had loved, was dead. And it was her fault.

Forcing her painful memories aside, Kerry looked at the house again, wondering whether to try the front door or go around the back. Flanking the house on both sides was a high stockade fence, and since she couldn't see any sign of a gate, she headed for

3

the front door. Kerry rang the bell and waited.

The house was quiet. Too quiet. She hesitated, then rang the bell again. Nothing. No sound from inside.

Just as she was wondering what to do, Kerry heard a voice calling for help. And then the sound of splashing water. Following the noises, she ran over to the side of the house. Then she heard it again, from the other side of the high fence.

"Help me out of the water, *please!*"

The fence was at least six feet high, and Kerry couldn't see over the top. She tried to climb it, but her feet kept slipping on the smooth wood. Then she spotted an old, rusted-out wheelbarrow propped up against the side of the house. She dragged it over to the fence, climbed on top, and peered into the yard.

A lone swimmer was slowly circling around a kidney-shaped swimming pool. It was a girl, a girl with long blond hair that streamed out behind her as she swam. And from what Kerry could see, it didn't look as if she was in any trouble.

Then, just as Kerry was about to call out to her, the girl in the pool raised an arm and called out again. "Help me out, *please*, Whitney."

"You don't need any help," came another voice.

Kerry squinted her eyes against the glare of the sun and saw the other girl. She was on horseback, about ten feet beyond the back fence.

"Don't be a pain, Whitney!" the girl in the pool yelled loudly. "Come and help me out."

"And get myself all wet? No way! I'm not falling for that trick again! The last time you said you needed help, you just wanted to pull me into the pool." With that, the girl wheeled her horse around. She dug her heels into its sides, and the animal reared up and lunged forward. In a flash she was gone.

Kerry tore her eyes away from the departing horse and rider and stared down at the swimmer in the pool. She was really puzzled. The blond girl was still swimming around quite easily, and from what Kerry could see, she appeared to be a strong swimmer. So why did she need help?

Crash!

"Garrummmphh!" Kerry yelled as she fell off the wheelbarrow.

"Who's there?" It was the girl in the pool.

"Kerry Logan," Kerry said between clenched teeth as she anxiously examined the scrape on her elbow. "I'm here for an interview."

There was a short silence. "Do you think you could climb the fence and help me out of the pool?"

"I don't know," Kerry answered, getting shakily to her feet. Her arm stung, and she rubbed the sore spot carefully. "I guess I could try."

"The fence is lower on the other side of the house!" the voice yelled back at her. "And please hurry."

Kerry managed to scramble over the fence, and she fell into the garden on the other side, crushing a clump of daisies that was growing there. She stumbled to her feet and started walking toward the pool, frowning with exasperation. It didn't make any sense. Why would someone who could swim like a fish need help getting out of a swimming pool?

Then a bell went off inside her head. Of course!

5

How could she have been so dumb? And there, parked on the grass under the shade of an enormous old oak tree, was a wheelchair. She hadn't seen it before, but it all made sense now.

Without thinking twice, or bothering to kick off her sneakers, Kerry waded down the steps and into the pool. The girl swam up to her, and Kerry reached down and put her arms around the girl's slim waist. She wasn't very heavy, and with a couple of heaves Kerry dragged her out of the water.

"Phew, thanks," the girl said a little breathlessly. "That was a close one. You've saved my life! Mom would kill me if she knew I'd gone swimming alone."

"Nothing to it," Kerry replied, feeling more than a little embarrassed. She waved toward the wheelchair. "Do you want me to help you into the chair?"

"No, I hate that miserable thing. I'll just sit by the edge for a while." The girl paused, and then reached out and touched Kerry's arm. "I'm Holly Chapman. My mother's the one who put the ad in the paper. She needs a watchdog for me, and I guess you can see why."

"If you can't get out of the pool by yourself, how on earth did you get in?" Kerry asked as she sat down.

"Getting in is easy. It's getting out that's the hard part," Holly replied ruefully. "I really thought I could do it, but my stupid legs won't work. They're useless."

"Why wouldn't that girl—the one on the horse— help you?" Kerry asked, suddenly remembering the horse and rider that had disappeared into the field beyond the garden.

"Oh, *her*," Holly replied with a grimace. "Miss

Whitney *Wonderful* Myers, the princess of Timber Ridge. She never helps anyone unless there's something in it for her. No, she's probably back at the barn by now telling my mother all about my crime. Look, I'd better get inside and dry off. Mom will be mad with me for swimming alone, and she'll be back any minute. Someone needed her at the stables, but she knows you're coming."

Kerry helped Holly into her wheelchair. She was impressed by the way the handicapped girl efficiently wheeled herself up the ramp and into the back door of the house.

"I'll be back out in a minute!" Holly yelled over her shoulder as she disappeared inside.

Kerry took off her wet sneakers and tried to squeeze some of the water out of them. Then she sat down on the wooden bench and waited for Mrs. Chapman, thinking that her job interview had started out in a really weird way.

"Oh, there you are, Kerry," a strange voice said.

Kerry looked up and saw a woman walking toward her across the grass. Mrs. Chapman looked remarkably like her daughter. Her hair was the same color of tawny, sun-streaked blond, except that it was short and wavy. A pair of friendly-looking blue eyes twinkled merrily in a suntanned face. She was wearing well-cut, buff-colored riding breeches, high black boots, and a white polo shirt. Kerry relaxed slightly, thinking that Holly's mother didn't look as if she was terribly upset by her daughter's recent escapade.

"Hi, I'm Liz Chapman," Holly's mother said. "Sorry I wasn't here when you arrived."

"That's okay," Kerry said quietly. "I haven't been here very long." And then she wondered if Mrs. Chapman really did know that Holly had been in the pool by herself.

As if reading her mind, Mrs. Chapman said, "You can probably guess why I advertised for a companion for Holly. She's much too headstrong for her own good, and being stuck in that wheelchair all the time makes her a little crazy. I'm just glad you were here to fish her out of the water before she turned into a shriveled prune."

Kerry giggled. Mrs. Chapman was nice. She crossed her fingers, hoping Holly's mother would like her well enough to offer her the job.

"Holly desperately needs company," Liz Chapman went on. "But I really had in mind someone older than you. By the way, how old are you, Kerry?"

"Thirteen and a half."

"Hmmm," Liz muttered thoughtfully. "Have you ever done anything like this before? Like baby-sitting, or looking after elderly people?"

Kerry shook her head. She'd never had any kind of a job before that wasn't connected with horses. And then she had a flash of inspiration. "I, er, sort of looked after my father, after my mom died. He's useless around the house."

"So am I," Liz admitted. "Can you cook?"

"Yes, but not very well," Kerry admitted.

"We're not fussy, and Holly hardly eats a thing," Liz said off-handedly. "I take it you can swim?"

Kerry nodded.

"Good, because with this heat wave we're having,

Holly spends most of her time in the pool. Swimming's the only form of exercise available to her, and her doctor recommended it highly to keep her leg muscles in shape."

Liz took a deep breath and stared toward the swimming pool. "Thank goodness this house already had a pool. I'd never have been able to afford to put one in for her," she said quietly. And then she paused again and looked closely at Kerry. "Even though you're much younger than I'd hoped for, I think I'll take a chance on you. But there's one more thing. If your father wouldn't object, I'd prefer that you come and live with us. It'd be easier that way, especially when I have to leave early in the morning to get to horse shows with the riding students."

"I'm living with my aunt, Molly Russell," Kerry explained. "My dad's in the Middle East on business and he probably won't be back till fall. I'd have to ask my aunt about it, but I don't think she'd mind."

"I'll phone her this evening," Liz said with a smile. "I'm sure she'll want to talk to me about it. If she agrees, I'd need you till school starts in September, okay?"

The word school made Kerry wonder if Holly went to school in Winchester or if she had to go to a special school for disabled kids. And then she wondered if Holly had always been in a wheelchair. She wanted to ask, but somehow it didn't seem quite right. But her curiosity got the better of her.

"Um, has Holly always . . . I mean . . ." Her voice trailed off in embarrassment.

"She was in a car accident," Liz Chapman said

quietly, sensing what Kerry was trying to ask. "Almost two years ago. Her father was driving, and"—there was a slight catch in her voice—"and he was killed. Holly hasn't been able to walk since."

"Will she ever walk again?"

"No one really knows," Liz answered slowly. "The doctors have assured me there's no permanent nerve damage, and they really don't know why she can't use her legs. One of them even suggested that it might be psychological. You know, something in Holly's mind that prevents her from walking. We've tried all sorts of cures, but so far, nothing's worked."

Just then Holly wheeled herself back outside. She'd changed into a bright pink sweat shirt, and her still-damp hair was tied back off her face. "Hey, Mom, did you hire her?" she asked with a grin as she joined them beside the pool.

"Yes," her mother replied, "but Kerry hasn't given me her answer yet." She turned toward the girl sitting beside her on the wooden bench. "Okay, Kerry, you've heard all about us. What do you think? Would you like the job?"

Kerry hesitated. Nothing that Liz had told her had included the stables. She had to make sure that the job didn't include being around the horses.

"Please say yes, Kerry," Holly said. "The last person Mom interviewed was straight out of *The Twilight Zone.*"

"Holly!" her mother said sternly, but her eyes were twinkling with amusement as she looked at Kerry. "What do you say?"

"Would I have to go to the stables?" Kerry blurted out.

"Oh, good. I'm glad you brought that up," Liz replied. "I almost forgot."

Kerry's heart sank.

Liz continued, "I can only afford to pay you fifteen dollars a week, plus your room and board, but to make up for the lack of money, I'll give you two or three riding lessons a week. Will that be okay?"

Kerry flinched.

"I know it's not much," Liz said, noticing Kerry's reaction, "but most girls your age love horses, so I figured you'd jump at the chance to ride."

"The money's fine," Kerry said quickly. "But I don't want the riding lessons."

"Kerry, don't you like horses?" Holly asked.

Kerry felt herself blushing. "Er, yes . . . I mean, no," she stammered out in a faltering voice.

"Holly, leave her alone," Liz said quickly, and then she put her hand reassuringly on Kerry's arm. "It's okay, Kerry. Don't be afraid to admit that you don't like horses. Not everyone's a horse-crazy maniac like Holly and me."

"I do like horses," Kerry admitted carefully. "But . . . but I'm scared of them." She hoped her lie was convincing enough to fool Holly and her mother.

Just then the phone rang. Liz excused herself and disappeared inside the house.

"I'm so glad you're going to do it," Holly said with enthusiasm. "I think we could have a lot of fun together, don't you, Kerry?"

Yes, Kerry thought to herself as she looked at Holly's cheerful smile. But only if she didn't have to go to the stables. She just wasn't ready for that.

Chapter Two

As the hot, noonday sun scorched down onto Kerry's already suntanned back, she drowsily decided that she'd fallen into the best job in the world. Here she was, lazing around a swimming pool, and being paid for keeping an eye on someone who she now considered her best friend.

This is perfect, she thought as she rolled over onto her back and reached for the magazine that Holly had been reading. It was a horse magazine—of course!

Rats! Kerry thought, and tossed the magazine aside. This would be the perfect job—if only she could chase away the terrible memories.

In the five days since Kerry had been living at the Chapmans' house, Holly had only gone to the stables once. And Liz had gone with her, leaving Kerry at the house with a stack of ironing. She hated ironing, but it was better than facing a barn full of horses.

Still, she knew it was only a matter of time before something else would come up, and Holly would want to go to the stables again, and she would have no excuse. She would have to go.

"Hey, Kerry," Holly called out as she swam toward the edge of the pool. "Come and help me out. I think I'm waterlogged."

Kerry hauled herself to her feet and went to help Holly out of the water. "Whew," she said as they both fell back on the grass, "I think you're heavier than you were the first time I did this."

"I am *not*," Holly sputtered indignantly, looking down at her trim waist and legs. And then she giggled. "But if I am, it's your fault. You shouldn't have made those brownies yesterday. You know, I think I ate most of them myself. They were terrific."

"I remember," Kerry said slyly. "You stuffed them down so fast, I thought you were going to choke!"

"It's the first time we've had brownies in the kitchen in years. Mom used to bake, but she doesn't have time anymore."

As Kerry settled herself back on the quilt, she glanced at the open pages of Holly's magazine. "You must really miss it," she said softly.

"What? Oh, riding." Holly's eyes grew sad. "Yeah, I really do. You know, sometimes I think I can really *feel* my legs wrapped around a horse as I'm taking off over a jump."

Kerry looked at her sympathetically. She wished she could say something that would make her friend feel better. Instead, she stared at the Chapmans' house. "I really love your house, Holly. You're so lucky to own it—it's so warm and comfortable."

"It's not ours," Holly said quietly. "It goes with Mom's job."

Kerry looked at her in astonishment. "Holly, if you don't own the house, and your Mom only runs the stables, then who really owns everything around here?"

"The almighty Timber Ridge Homeowners' Association. They also own the golf course, the tennis courts, the swimming pool, *and* the stables. The only thing they don't own is the ski area."

"So who owns that?"

"The Armstrongs. You'll get to meet Sue Armstrong this afternoon. She's such a terrific rider, Mom lets her use Magician."

"Why will I meet her this afternoon?" Kerry asked, not too sure that she was going to like the answer. "And who's Magician?"

Holly grinned. "He's my horse. You'll love him. Everybody does. He's so big, and yet very gentle. He's got the sweetest eyes in the world, and he jumps like a kangaroo!"

A feeling of dread passed through Kerry as Holly continued. "Mom wants us to come and watch her team practicing this afternoon. They're getting ready for a big horse show next month, and Mom's really sweating it."

"Why?" Kerry asked, trying not to think about going to the barn with Holly.

"Because if she doesn't produce riders who bring home blue ribbons all the time, her contract to manage the stables might not be renewed for next year.

She's worried stiff, but I know she'll make it. She *has* to."

For a moment Kerry forgot all about having to visit the stables. "Holly, that's *awful*," she cried.

"I know. It stinks," Holly muttered miserably. "Everything was fine until Mrs. Myers got involved. Before that, Mom ran the stables the way *she* wanted. The kids had lots of fun, and nobody cared if they won or lost. Just as long as they had a good time and learned how to take care of their horses."

"Is Mrs. Myers *that* bad?"

"Even worse," Holly said with a scowl. "She makes Godzilla look like Kermit the Frog."

Kerry burst out laughing.

"Just wait till you meet her," Holly warned. "You'll see what I mean. She's the worst kind of horse-show mother, and sometimes I even feel sorry for Whitney!"

Kerry shot her a puzzled glance. "Huh?"

"She's always on Whitney's back about winning. If she doesn't bring home tons of trophies and blue ribbons, Mrs. Myers has an absolute fit." Then she grinned. "Come on, let's go to the stables and see how Mom's doing with the team."

Kerry forced herself to smile and started to gather up their things. She helped Holly into her chair and gave her the magazine and a pile of towels to hold on her knees.

"Hey, Kerry, look at this," Holly squealed in excitement. She pointed to a picture at the top of the page. "That kid's just like *me*," she whispered. "See the wheelchair? And he's wearing leg braces as well."

Kerry peered over her shoulder. Quickly she read

the caption beside the photograph:

Ten-year-old Tim Sullivan can ride his pony even though he's handicapped, thanks to the efforts of the volunteers at the Vermont Riding for the Handicapped Association.

"That does it!" Holly said in a determined voice. "If 'Tiny Tim' can do it, so can I. Come on, Kerry. Let's go and find Mom. I want to show her this."

She turned around and stared at Kerry's strained expression. "Don't worry," she added kindly. "The horses won't hurt you. It's not as if they're running wild all over the place. We do keep them penned up most of the time."

Kerry tried to smile at Holly's joke, but it wasn't easy. Her stomach was churning over and over, and she could feel the sweat on her hands where they gripped the handles of the wheelchair.

"I'm okay," she lied.

Whitney Myers turned her horse around and looked toward her mother. Mrs. Myers was leaning against her silver Mercedes on the other side of the rails. Having her mother watch her practice made Whitney nervous, and she wished she'd stay away.

"Okay, Whitney!" Liz yelled from the middle of the ring. "I want you to take the parallel bars again. And this time don't keep such a tight rein. Let Astronaut have his head. He knows what he's doing."

Whitney cringed at the criticism, knowing her mother would ask her about it later. She always got the third-degree treatment after a riding team practice.

She tightened her legs around Astronaut's sides

and twisted her fingers through the reins. The jump was almost four feet, and it looked enormous. "Don't you dare refuse," she whispered urgently as the big bay horse started cantering toward the red and white jump. He'd run out on it the first time she'd tried, and she was determined he was going to jump. With Mother watching her, she'd better get him over it, one way or the other.

"Who's that?" Kerry asked as she helped Holly steer her wheelchair over the bumpy ground toward the riding ring. Her heart was beating almost as loud as the horse's thundering hooves as he flashed by them. She stopped and held her breath as the horse and rider soared over the parallel bars.

"Princess Whitney Myers," Holly said scornfully.

"Is she the girl who wouldn't help you out of the pool?"

Holly nodded. "Yes."

"Is she a good rider?" Kerry winced as Whitney jerked her horse to a stop at the far end of the ring.

Holly frowned. "Yes . . . and no. She's good because her horse, Astronaut, is what you'd call 'push-button.' You just sit there, push the right buttons, and he performs."

Kerry tried to act dumb. "And Whitney knows how to push buttons?"

"Yeah, but that's about all. She only bothers to ride when she's got an audience. She refuses to really work at her riding, or anything else, for that matter. She always gets someone else to do the dirty work for her. Like grooming her horse, or cleaning his stall. All the other kids help out, but not Princess Whitney."

18

Liz waved at them. Then she turned and spoke to another girl who was on a chestnut horse with a white star on its forehead. The girl cantered up to the jump, and for a moment it looked as if her horse was going to refuse. She kicked him once, and he popped over it like a cat.

"Good, you kept him going, Robin," Liz said approvingly. Then she turned to the last horse. "This one shouldn't give you any trouble, Susan. Go ahead."

"That's Magician," Holly said proudly as the big black horse thundered toward the jump. "Was I right, or is he gorgeous?"

Kerry let out an involuntary gasp as she stared at Holly's horse. For a moment she thought her mind was playing tricks on her. It couldn't be!

Chapter Three

Kerry's thoughts whirled back in time. She shook her head, trying to banish the painful memory that had just come back to haunt her.

She blinked twice and looked at the horse again. The resemblance was frightening. Magician looked *exactly* like Black Magic! The same proud head with small ears pricked forward, the arched neck, and the short, well-muscled body that ended in powerful hindquarters and a long, flowing tail. The only difference between them was that Black Magic had had a small white star in the middle of his forehead. Otherwise, the two horses were identical.

Even their names were similar—Magician . . . Black Magic. It was weird, and Kerry felt as if it were some sort of an omen. But, whether it was a good or bad omen, she couldn't tell.

It took all of Kerry's willpower to stay at the ring, watching the rest of the lesson. She wanted to run away and hide from the big black horse. He was a frightening reminder of something she was trying hard to forget.

"Okay, kids, that's enough for today," Liz called out loudly. "Take your horses inside, and don't forget to walk them out. They're all sweating, and go easy on their water."

The horses left the ring, and Liz walked toward the fence. Her face looked strained and tired, and Kerry felt sorry for her. It wasn't fair. Riding horses and entering competitions was supposed to be fun. At least, it had been for her until—she angrily pushed the thought aside and tried to smile.

"Mom!" Holly cried as Liz climbed over the fence. "You've gotta read this." She shoved the magazine toward her mother. "There's an article in here about handicapped kids who are *riding*!"

Liz smiled and nodded. "I know. I've read it."

"What?" Holly exploded. "And you didn't tell me?"

"No, I didn't."

"But why, Mom? It sounds great. I want to try. You should have said something to me."

"I'm sorry, Holly. I thought you'd hate it. I mean, most of the kids in this program have never ridden before. You have, and it won't be the same. You'd only get frustrated and end up hating it."

"No, I wouldn't," Holly said, shaking her head vigorously. "Please let me try. I'd give anything to ride Magician again."

"Uh-uh, Holly. He's quiet and well mannered, but not for this kind of thing. He needs a strong pair of legs around him. You ought to know that."

"What about Hobo, then?" Holly insisted. "Surely he wouldn't mind if I rode him. He's as quiet as a mouse."

"It might work," Liz agreed slowly. "But I can't do this for you without some help."

"So call them, Mom. Their phone number's at the end of the article."

Liz smiled affectionately. "Okay, then, if you insist. I'll see if I can get one of their volunteers to come and show me what to do. But I'll still need someone else to help me as well." She looked toward Kerry.

"I can't," Kerry whispered. "I'm sorry, but . . . I'm scared. They're . . . so big." She hated herself for the lie.

"That's okay, Kerry," Liz said kindly. "I guess one of the other kids can give us a hand. All I ask is that you help Holly get herself over here, and we'll take care of everything else." She paused and looked at Kerry's flushed face. "Don't be embarrassed, Kerry. I admire you for having the guts to admit you're afraid. Most people would try to bluff it out and end up in trouble."

Holly reached out and grabbed Kerry's arm, pulling her toward the chair. "Please come and see Magician with me," she said. "He'll be in his stall by now, and you can look at him through the bars. I want to give him a carrot and tell him I still love him. Okay?"

Kerry mutely agreed and started pushing the wheelchair toward the barn. As she got closer, the familiar smell of horses and fresh-cut hay drifted toward her. This was the first time she'd been inside

23

a stable since Black Magic had died. She didn't know how she was going to react.

"Come on, Kerry," Holly said impatiently. "Let's go and see Magician."

Once she was actually inside the barn, Kerry felt numb. No feeling of shock, or even guilt. Just numb. She just hoped she'd stay that way long enough to get through the next half hour.

As Holly pointed out the tackroom, the grain storage area, and her mother's small office, Kerry walked along the cement aisle not daring to look anywhere but straight ahead. Out of the corners of her eyes, she could see familiar sights—rakes and pitchforks leaning against the walls, half-empty water buckets, the contents of someone's grooming box that had spilled onto the sawdust-covered floor. Things she knew and had loved so well in the past, but things that could only hurt her now. If only it hadn't happened. If only she had checked that stall door.

"Here we are." Holly interrupted Kerry's thoughts. "You can let go of me now, Kerry. Why don't you just wait out here and look at him through the bars. Oh, there's Susan." She wheeled herself into the stall. "Hi, he looked great out there."

Kerry stood back and watched as Holly held out her hand with the carrot. Magician gently nuzzled his soft nose into her palm and accepted his treat.

"Hi, there. You must be Kerry." A short, sandy-haired girl walked up to her. She had been brushing the black horse, and she grinned at Kerry from inside the stall. "I'm Susan Armstrong. Holly's told me all about you. Why don't you come inside and join the party. I don't think Magician will mind another guest."

Kerry shook her head. "No, thanks," she muttered, wishing with all her heart that she could forget all her problems and run right into the horse's stall.

"Hey, Susan," Holly said, "Kerry's not too fond of horses. She's better off out there."

"Okay," Susan said. "Nice to meet you." She went back to the horse and started brushing him vigorously.

Just then Kerry felt someone come up behind her.

"Holly, aren't you going to introduce me to your new slave?" an icy voice questioned.

Kerry turned around abruptly and found herself staring into a pair of penetrating pale blue eyes, framed by a creamy white face and masses of very dark hair. In spite of the fact that it was hot and sticky, Whitney Myers looked as if she'd just stepped out of an advertisement for Devon-Aire riding clothes. Her pale yellow shirt was spotless, and her white riding breeches didn't look as if she'd just spent a grueling hour on the back of a horse. Even her black boots were polished and shiny.

Holly ignored the jibe. "Aren't you supposed to be brushing your horse?" she said sharply as she wheeled herself toward the stall door.

Whitney shrugged. "Monica's doing it for me. Besides, he wasn't *that* sweaty."

Just as Holly opened her mouth in an angry retort, Magician, tired of being ignored, pushed past her and tried to join the conversation.

25

"Get back in your stall, you silly horse!" Holly cried as the animal tried to squeeze his way past her chair.

Kerry jumped, then fell back against the wall, pretending to be afraid of the oncoming horse.

Her sudden movement didn't escape Whitney's scornful eyes. "What's the matter? Scared of a big pussycat like Magician, are you?"

"Leave her alone," Holly snapped. She'd managed to grab on to the horse's halter and was shoving him back where he'd come from.

Kerry wished the floor would crack wide open and swallow her up right then. She felt dumb, cringing against the wall. But now that she'd started to pretend she was afraid, there was no going back.

"Whitney, why is Monica brushing *your* horse?" Liz's voice interrupted. She was walking briskly down the aisle checking on the horses, holding a bridle in her hands. "And I found this, lying on the ground outside Astronaut's stall. I believe it's yours." With a stony expression she handed the bridle to Whitney.

"Ugh, it's got manure all over it," Whitney said with disgust, refusing to touch it.

"What do you expect?" Liz retorted. "It was flung on the ground. I suggest you clean it immediately. *After* you take care of your horse."

"My mother's waiting for me," Whitney said nonchalantly. "We have guests coming for dinner. Why don't you find someone else to clean it for me? I'll see you tomorrow." With that, she flicked her hair away from her face and strode off, not even bothering to look at her horse as she passed by his stall.

"Can you believe that?" Susan gasped incredulously. "My mother would murder me if she thought I acted like that. What a creep!"

"Susan, would you mind hanging this up in the tackroom for me?" Liz handed her the dirty bridle. "And don't you dare feel sorry for her and end up cleaning it," she warned her sternly. "She can ride with a dirty bridle tomorrow, and maybe she'll learn something. Although I doubt it."

Kerry's nerves were almost at breaking point, and she wished Holly would hurry up and finish cuddling her horse. Just when she felt like screaming out loud, Holly wheeled herself out of Magician's stall. "I'm all finished," she said cheerfully. "Let's go back home and have another swim."

Once outside, Kerry took a deep lungful of fresh air and trembled with relief. It was over, and it hadn't been quite as bad as she'd expected.

"Whitney's still here," Holly said as they made their way past the riding ring.

Kerry glanced toward the Mercedes and saw that Whitney and her mother were arguing loudly.

"Of course I'll be on the team, Mother," Whitney said angrily as she opened the car door. "You know I'm the best rider they've got."

"I hope so," Mrs. Myers answered in a cool voice. "I paid a fortune for that horse of yours, and your father and I will be very disappointed in you if you don't win at the Hampshire Classic."

"I'll win," Whitney snapped. She glared at Kerry as she climbed into the car, slamming the door shut behind her.

"I think you've just been added to Whitney's 'hit

27

list,'" Holly whispered as the large silver Mercedes purred out of the driveway.

"Why? I didn't even say anything to her."

"I know, but you were there when Mom told her off. And you just heard her arguing with her mother. She won't forgive you for that," Holly warned.

Kerry shrugged. "Well, I guess I'll just have to keep out of her way, then."

"I don't see how you can. You'll be bringing me to the barn almost every day from now on," Holly replied.

Right, Kerry thought to herself. She only hoped she could handle it.

Liz had made arrangements with a volunteer from Riding for the Handicapped to come to the barn the next day. And as she left for the stables early that morning, she reminded Kerry to bring Holly over at three o'clock. There was no way Kerry could refuse.

Her stomach was tied up in knots by the time they reached the barn, and she had to force herself to go inside. Quickly she helped Holly wheel her chair to the stable area, where Liz took over. Then she ran outside, settled herself underneath a tree, and tried to read.

But it was no good. She kept thinking about Holly, wondering what she was feeling—riding a horse again! Then she started to feel ashamed. Holly was trying to overcome a really serious problem, and she was too scared to even go and watch! Angrily Kerry forced her attention back to the book, but the words blurred before her eyes. She stared at the same page for ten minutes, then jumped to her feet. She wasn't a coward! She *would* go and watch!

Quietly she walked into the indoor riding ring and hid herself in the shadows. Holly was up on the pony really riding. Slowly, of course. Liz walked on one side, and the volunteer, Anne Norton, walked on the other. And from the look of joy on Holly's face, it was obvious she was in seventh heaven.

"Mom, I'm riding again!" Holly cried breathlessly. "I can't believe it."

"That's it, Holly," Anne Norton said cheerfully. "Try and feel the rhythm of the pony as he walks. Let your body relax and move with him."

Liz smiled happily at her daughter's ecstatic face and patted her on the leg. "Let me walk with her, Anne. I'd like you to stand back and tell me if we're doing it right."

"Do you think I'll be ready for the next Olympics?" Holly asked with a grin.

"Not till you can jump the double oxer without your stirrups, young lady," Anne replied firmly.

"That comes *next* week!" Holly joked.

At the end of the lesson Holly was so excited she couldn't stop talking about it.

"Kerry, you've no idea what it feels like," she said after Anne had left. "You've *got* to take riding lessons. Just think how much fun we could have if we were both riding together!" She leaned forward and rubbed her hand up and down the pony's neck.

Kerry didn't trust herself to answer. She was light-years away from riding a horse again! But being at the barn wasn't as painful as she had expected, and as she followed Liz and the pony back to the stables, she felt some of the old excitement returning.

One day, about a week later, when Holly had finished her lesson, Kerry found herself standing outside Magician's stall. The horse pricked his ears forward and whinnied softly at her.

"I think he likes you," Liz said with a smile as she passed by, leading Hobo into his stall.

"He's beautiful," Kerry murmured as she stared through the bars at the big black horse. Now that she knew him better, he didn't remind her so painfully of Black Magic. He'd taken on his own personality, and she found herself drawn toward him. He was like a magnet, and she couldn't keep away.

"Are you *sure* you don't want to start riding lessons?" Liz inquired. She closed Hobo's stall door and looked closely at Kerry.

Kerry wanted to yell YES at the top of her voice. Instead, she said, "No, thanks. I'll just watch."

The next day Whitney and her best friend, Monica Blake, showed up in the middle of Holly's riding lesson. They'd been playing tennis, and both of them were stylishly dressed in short white tennis dresses. Whitney was carrying an expensive-looking tennis racket under her arm.

"I see the country-club set has just turned up," Holly muttered to Kerry as she rode by on the pony.

Kerry turned around and saw them. Instinctively she moved farther away. Just as Holly had predicted, Whitney never missed an opportunity to make fun

30

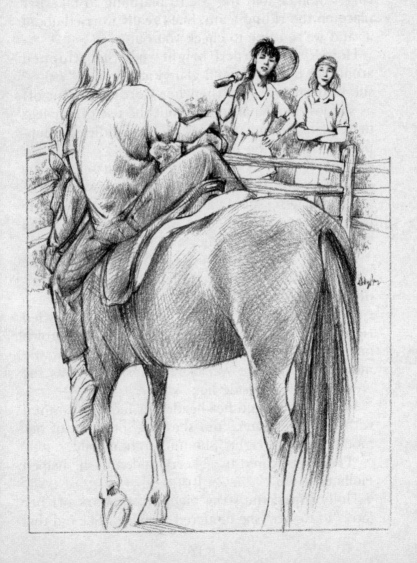

of her, and she wasn't in the mood for any more of her spiteful tongue.

"Hey, Holly," Whitney called out across the riding ring. "Monica told me you're planning to take her place on the riding team. She's really worried about it, and we've come to check you out."

Holly's face turned bright red. She whipped around in the saddle and glared at Whitney. "You—" she blurted out, and then her words were cut off as she lost her balance. Without the use of her legs to keep her firmly planted in the saddle, she toppled slowly off the pony's back.

"Holly!" Kerry cried out. For a split second she couldn't move. Holly was lying perfectly still on the ground where she'd landed, and for a horrible moment Kerry thought she was unconscious. Then she pulled herself together and ran toward her.

Liz, who'd been checking some loose boards at the far end of the ring, heard the cries and came running from the other direction.

Kerry breathlessly rushed up to Holly's sprawled figure. She was lying face down on the soft brown tanbark that covered the indoor arena, and she wasn't moving. "Holly, are you okay?" Kerry cried as she crouched down beside her.

Holly slowly lifted her head. Her face was covered with bits of tanbark, and she spat some out of her mouth. "I'm all right," she muttered angrily.

"Phew, you scared me," Kerry said, and she helped Holly to sit up.

Holly wiped the stray pieces of tanbark off her face. "I *hate* her," she muttered viciously. "She did that on purpose. If I could walk, I'd go over there right now and wring her neck."

Kerry put her arm around Holly's shoulders. "I don't think Whitney meant for you to fall off."

"Holly, are you all right?" Liz led the pony up to them and looked anxiously at her daughter. "You're not hurt, are you?"

"I'm okay, Mom," Holly said in a tight voice. "But I've had enough for today. Could someone get my chair for me?"

"I'll go." Kerry got up and ran across the ring. She glanced toward Whitney and Monica and was gratified to see that they looked very embarrassed. Good, she thought as she entered the stables. Serves them right for being so stupid!

She found Holly's chair outside the tackroom. Just as she was about to push it back into the arena, she hesitated, and then stopped. Slowly she turned around and approached Magician's stall. He heard her coming and whinnied.

"You beautiful horse," Kerry murmured quietly. She reached for the latch on his stall door, then hesitated. Could she do it?

With trembling fingers, she pulled the latch free, and the door swung slowly open. Magician whinnied again and shuffled forward to nuzzle her hand. "Sorry, boy," she said softly. "I don't have anything for you."

Hesitantly Kerry put her arms around his neck. She felt his strength and warmth flooding through her. His wonderful horsy smell tickled her nose, and she pressed herself even closer. As she leaned against

33

him, a plan started to take shape in the back of her mind. It was time to forget the past, and she knew that somehow Magician would help her.

But it was something she needed to do alone. She couldn't share it with anyone. Not even Holly.

Chapter Four

Now that Kerry had dealt with her first problem—facing horses again—another one cropped up. To do what she had planned required privacy. She couldn't afford the risk of being seen.

The opportunity she'd been waiting for occurred the following Friday evening. Right after dinner Holly announced contentedly, "I don't feel like riding tonight, Mom. I ate too much."

"Good," Liz replied, "because I want to get to bed early. I have to leave before six in the morning, and if you girls don't mind clearing up the mess we've made, I think I'll turn in."

Kerry's heart jumped. This is it, she thought as she picked up the glasses and plates from the picnic table and took them into the kitchen. As Holly brought in some more behind her, Kerry rinsed them off and started to load the dishwasher. Now all she had to do was convince Holly that she needed to go out for a while—alone—and she could get on with her plan.

"Holly, I think I'll ride my bike down to the village and visit Aunt Molly," she said casually, hoping that Holly wouldn't object to being alone for the evening.

"Everyone's deserting me," Holly said with a grimace. And then she smiled. "Say hi to your aunt for me, okay? And do you want me to leave the front door unlocked for you?"

Kerry shook her head. "I won't be late. I'll probably be back around ten or so." She left Holly sitting at the kitchen table and ran into her bedroom to change. This was going to be the tricky part—getting out of the house without letting Holly see that she'd changed into jeans and riding boots.

She pulled off her shorts and slipped into a pair of jeans. Then she took the riding boots out of her closet. She'd found them in Holly's bedroom, buried underneath a pile of old clothes and boxes on the top shelf of Holly's closet. She struggled into them with difficulty. They were a bit on the tight side, but since she wasn't planning on taking a ten-mile hike in them, she decided they'd suit her purpose very well.

For five minutes she hung around her room, waiting for the right moment. It came when the telephone rang. Kerry dashed into Holly's bedroom and grabbed the extension. It was Susan Armstrong.

"Hey, Holly—Susan's on the phone!" Kerry shouted.

"I'll take it in the kitchen!" Holly yelled back. "Hi, Sue. What's up?"

Kerry slipped out the door without being seen.

36

The stables were deserted, except for the horses and the small herd of barn cats that inhabited the hayloft. One of them meowed noisily and curled its furry body around her ankle. Kerry bent down and scratched its head. Thank goodness Liz doesn't have any lessons tonight, she said to herself as she made her way to the tackroom, the cat skittering along behind her.

She hit the main light switch and blinked as all the lights came on at once. Hoping no one would notice that the barn was lit up like a Christmas tree, Kerry picked up Holly's grooming box and pulled Magician's saddle and bridle off their pegs.

Magician was half-asleep, and he snorted with surprise when he saw Kerry outside his stall. Recognizing her, he whinnied softly and nuzzled her outstretched hand, hoping for a carrot.

"Not tonight, old boy," Kerry said quietly, feeling sorry that she hadn't been able to sneak any carrots out of the refrigerator for him.

She took a deep breath and felt her hand tremble as she curled her fingers around the wooden brush. Slowly she drew it across Magician's shoulders, then down his foreleg. His coat was so shiny—and black! A distorted vision of Black Magic came into her mind, and she blinked back a tear.

Her brushstrokes grew stronger; and as she worked, she started to relax. It had been months since she'd groomed a horse, and oh, how she'd missed it!

Magician whinnied with pleasure, and his velvety coat gleamed with good health. Then she switched brushes and started on his mane, gently sorting out the tangles, until it lay gracefully on his neck. She wished she could go on grooming him all night, but the moment had finally arrived. It was time to tack him up and get on with her plan.

Gently she held the bridle in front of his head and slipped the soft rubber snaffle into his mouth. As Magician chewed on the bit, Kerry eased the bridle over his ears and adjusted the straps. Then she carefully placed Holly's saddle on his back and did up his girth.

Once in the indoor arena her nerve almost deserted her. Maybe this wasn't such a good idea after all.

Magician seemed to sense her hesitation. He swung his head around and nudged her playfully. He seemed to be saying, "Get on with it."

"I'm gonna do it!" Kerry said in a determined voice, and before she had a chance to change her mind, she vaulted into the saddle in one fluid movement.

For a few minutes she just sat there, hardly daring to breathe. She'd done it! She was in the saddle again! Then as her confidence grew, she gently tightened her hold on the reins and squeezed Magician's sides with her legs. He walked forward, and tremors of excitement ran up and down Kerry's spine.

His stride was relaxed and easy, and Kerry felt the tension leave her body as he walked across the ring. "I can't believe it," she said softly, leaning forward to rub her hand up and down his neck. "I'm riding again!"

After one turn around the ring, she urged him into

a slow trot. At first she sat quietly in the saddle, marveling at the horse's easy gait. Then she squeezed her legs again and trotted faster, posting up and down instead of sitting still.

The exhilaration she felt as Magician lengthened his stride made her want to laugh and cry at the same time. "You terrific horse!" she said loudly. Magician answered her with a flick of his ears.

"Okay, let's canter!" Magician needed no further urging. Without missing a beat, he broke into a slow, collected canter. "You're just like a rocking chair!" Kerry said softly as her body swayed rhythmically back and forth in time with the horse's smooth movements.

She didn't want to stop. She could go on cantering him in circles all night, but the jumps were beckoning to her. Did she dare? Was she brave enough to jump?

Kerry felt her stomach muscles tighten with tension as she stared at the brightly colored jumps scattered around the ring. She had to try. Unless she did, the cure wouldn't be complete. But could she really do it?

Magician seemed to sense her anxiety because he slowed down and came to a stop in the middle of the ring. Kerry stared with glassy eyes at the small cross-rail. It was right in front of her, and all she had to do was gently squeeze Magician's sides with her legs.

"I can do it!" she said grimly. Without giving herself a chance to back down, she urged the horse into a trot. As the tiny jump drew closer, Kerry wanted to pull him away. She tightened her grip on the saddle and felt her hands pulling on the reins. But Magician ignored her, and with one graceful motion he jumped the cross-rail.

"Wow!" Kerry exclaimed when they landed safely on the other side. "I did it!" She leaned forward and patted the horse's neck. Magician turned his head around and flicked his ears. Kerry smiled, her confidence increased.

She urged Magician into a slow canter and glanced toward the brush jump. It was only three feet high, and as they cantered past it, Kerry's determination hardened. "This one next," she whispered to her horse, and she turned him around to face the jump.

The horse needed no further urging. He sprang forward and in three strides cleared the brush jump. Kerry thought she was going to burst from excitement. She was so caught up in the wondrous feeling of jumping again that she forgot to check her horse. He kept on going, and before she realized, they were approaching the parallel bars.

Kerry instinctively leaned forward into Magician's neck and saw the red and white poles flashing by underneath them. He must have cleared it by at least a foot; and when they landed safely on the other side, Kerry cried out loud. "I'm cured! I'm not scared anymore!"

Her face broke into an ecstatic smile, and she leaned forward and wrapped her arms around Magician's neck. "Thank you, thank you," she whispered into his mane.

* * *

Holly put the phone down just as Liz's old grandfather clock struck a single note. She rubbed her ear thoughtfully. She and Sue had spent over an hour on the phone. Kerry would be back soon.

She opened the front door and wheeled herself outside. The night air smelled sweet and fresh. She decided to go and meet Kerry on her way back from the village. Just as she reached the end of the garden path, a faint gleam of light caught her eye.

Holly blinked and looked again. She wasn't mistaken. Someone had left the barn lights on.

"I'd better check it out," she muttered. But as she got closer to the barn doors, she knew it wasn't just a light left accidentally on. From the rhythmic pounding that was coming from inside, she knew someone was riding.

Holly quietly opened the small side door and wheeled herself inside. Filled with curiosity, she went another few feet until she reached a gap in the wall that surrounded the indoor arena. She peered around the corner and gasped.

For a split second Holly was stunned. What on earth was Susan Armstrong doing, riding Magician so late at night? It had to be her—no one else was allowed to ride him.

Then Holly became alarmed. She'd just gotten off the phone with Sue ten minutes ago. There was no way she could have had time to get down to the stables, saddle him up, and start riding.

So if it wasn't Susan Armstrong, who on earth was the mysterious rider who was so expertly riding Magician over the jumping course?

Chapter Five

"Kerry Logan, you're a liar!" Holly's voice suddenly erupted in the silence of the barn.

Startled beyond belief, Kerry almost fell off the horse. Awkwardly she pulled herself back into the saddle and looked toward the sound of the voice. All at once, the joy that she had felt at riding again vanished. As she stared into Holly's angry face, she knew she was going to have to tell her the truth. It was something she didn't want to do. Not yet. Not until she'd had time to sort things out for herself.

"Why didn't you tell us you could ride?" Holly asked. She sounded miserable as well as angry. "Why did you lie and pretend to be afraid?"

Kerry gulped and felt herself turning bright red. "Holly, I'm sorry," she blurted out. "I didn't mean to hurt you, or Liz. Honest, I didn't." The words sounded hollow, and she felt ashamed of all the lies that she'd told.

"Why don't you put my horse back in his stall, and then we'll talk," Holly said in a cold, hard voice. Without looking in Kerry's direction, she wheeled herself along the passageway beside the arena and disappeared into the tackroom.

Five minutes later Kerry joined her. She put Magician's saddle and bridle back on their pegs, and then she sat down on a tack trunk. Her heart was beating wildly, and she was feeling miserable. Finally she forced herself to look at Holly.

"You know," Holly said slowly, her blue eyes staring harshly at Kerry, "right now, I think I hate you as much as I hate Whitney Myers. Maybe even more. At least I know what she's like. I *know* what to expect from her. But you—" Her voice choked off angrily. "I thought you were my friend, Kerry."

"I *am* your friend, Holly," Kerry replied in a whisper. "Please believe me, please!"

"If you're my friend, why didn't you trust me with the truth?"

"Because I was too ashamed," Kerry muttered.

"Ashamed of what?" Holly demanded. "Of being able to ride? That's stupid, Kerry."

Kerry took a deep breath. "Okay," she said slowly and carefully. "I guess I do owe you the truth, but before I begin, I want you to promise me something."

Holly's eyes narrowed. "What?"

"That you won't tell your mother."

"Why?"

"You'll understand when I tell you. Please promise."

Holly hesitated. "Okay," she said reluctantly.

"I used to ride at a place called Sandpiper Sta-

44

bles," Kerry said slowly, trying to control her wavering voice. "There was a horse there—his name was Black Magic, and he was the best one they'd ever had. Mrs. Mueller, the owner, had trained him from a foal, and this summer she was going to let me ride him in some three-day events." She paused and blinked several times, hoping she would be able to talk about it without crying.

"Go on," Holly said quietly.

"Besides being a terrific jumper, Black Magic was a terribly smart horse. He could get out of his stall, and almost any field we put him in. He'd either undo the latch, or else he'd jump out. I used to work at the stables because I couldn't afford lessons unless I did; and one night, after I'd fed all the horses, Black Magic got out of his stall."

"Didn't you, or Mrs. Mueller, try to barricade him in with something?" Holly interrupted. "One of our horses used to be like that, and we had to put a padlock on his stall door."

"Oh, yes," Kerry replied. "We had all sorts of tricks to keep him in." She hesitated and stared miserably at Holly.

"And so he got out," Holly prompted. "Was he hurt?"

Kerry couldn't stop the tears that started to trickle down her face. "He got into the feed room and gorged himself on the sweet feed. Mrs. Mueller heard the noise from her house, came out, and dragged him back into his stall."

"Then what happened?"

"She called the vet, but it was too late. Black Magic

45

got colic, and he died the next morning. There was nothing they could do to save him." Kerry's voice broke, and suddenly she began to sob.

A rush of pity came over Holly. She clumsily wheeled herself over to the miserable girl. "Don't, don't," she said gently, and reached out to touch Kerry's hand.

"I'm sorry," Kerry said with a gulp. "I can't help it. You see, they blamed *me*. I was the last one in his stall that night, and I didn't close his door tightly enough. Now he's dead, and it's all my fault."

"You can't blame yourself forever," Holly murmured softly. "It was an accident. You said he was a wizard at getting out. Maybe you did do his door up, but he somehow figured out how to get it undone."

Kerry shook her head. "No, I must have forgotten to put the padlock on," she said in a whisper. "I was in a rush that night. Dad was waiting for me. He'd just heard about his latest job assignment, and we were going to talk about what I would do while he was gone. Mrs. Mueller had invited me to stay with her until he got back. She used to treat me like one of the family. Until . . ." She couldn't go on.

"But why did you tell us you couldn't ride?" Holly asked. "Why did you pretend to be scared of horses?"

"Because of what happened," Kerry said in an anguished voice. "Don't you see? Black Magic died, and it was all my fault. After it happened, I just couldn't face another horse."

"Did they *really* blame you?" Holly asked suddenly. "Or did you only *think* they did?"

Kerry wiped her eyes. "Oh, they blamed me, all

right. Mrs. Mueller was furious. When I got to the barn that morning, she yelled at me to come into the house immediately. She'd never yelled at me before, and I had no idea what was wrong. And then she hit me with it. Her first words were, 'Magic is dead, and *you* killed him!'"

"She sounds horrible," Holly said sharply.

"She wasn't," Kerry said quickly. "I told you. She used to treat me like one of the family."

"So why did she accuse *you* of killing the horse?"

"Because I *did*. No one else was at the stables that night, and she trusted me to make sure everything was okay before I left. That was part of my job, and I blew it."

"Couldn't someone else have gone into his stall after you left?" Holly asked.

"No, I was the last one there that night." Kerry sighed and shook her head.

"Um, Kerry," Holly said in a tight voice. "I'm sorry I was so awful to you. I didn't mean what I said about hating you more than Whitney. Will you forgive me?"

Kerry smiled weakly. "Of course I will. And promise not to tell Liz. Okay?"

"All right, but I don't understand why. You know how much she likes you. Why won't you let me tell her? You're really good, you know, and I'm sure she'd jump at the chance of having you on the team."

Kerry shook her head violently. "No," she said urgently. "I don't want anyone to know what happened. It was bad enough telling you. I don't think I could bear it if anyone else knew. Just let me get used to riding again. With you to help me, maybe I can practice a little more on Magician; and after I've ridden him a few more times, I'll tell her myself."

"Okay, you win," Holly said grudgingly. "I'll give you a week. I'm sure that between us we can figure out enough excuses to get down here when no one else is around. But, we'll have to be careful. The last thing we need is for Whitney or Monica to see you ride. That would really mess things up, but good!"

"Oh boy, look how late it is," Kerry said as she checked her watch. "If your mother wakes up and finds out we're not in the house, she'll have a fit."

They turned off the lights and left the barn, talking about horses and riding. As they hurried home, neither girl was aware of someone standing in the shadows.

Another pair of eyes had witnessed Kerry's ride. Pale blue eyes that were now angry. Angry . . . and dangerous!

Whitney let out a gasp of horror as she emerged from her hiding place in the feed room. And just think! If she hadn't gone back to get her radio, she'd never have known about Kerry Logan's terrible secret.

For a moment her mind was in a whirl, and she couldn't think straight. Visions of Kerry and Magician soaring expertly over the jumping course flashed before her. As she got herself under control, Whitney knew she had a serious problem. If Liz Chapman saw Kerry ride, it would mean the end of Whitney's star position on the riding team. And that was something she could never let happen. There was no way she was going to lose out to a nobody like Kerry Logan!

Chapter Six

"Okay," Holly said patiently, "let's go over this again. Just to be sure we've got our stories straight. We both have to say the same thing."

Kerry smiled at Holly's anxious face. She was glad that she'd decided to go along with her about telling Liz everything. Well, not quite everything. And Holly was right. They had to make sure they both said the same thing.

Holly continued. "The reason you didn't tell anyone you could ride was that you'd had an accident and were scared. Let's see." She paused and frowned. "Oh, yes. You were riding a horse . . . quick, think of a name for me."

"Secret Agent," Kerry suggested with a silly grin.

Holly almost choked. "Ugh," she said between giggles. "You've been reading too many spy stories. Come on, be serious. A name. Anything will do, just as long as we both remember it."

"Okay. Hot Shot," Kerry said quickly, using the name of the pony she'd learned to ride on.

"Good," Holly replied. "Okay, then, you were riding this horse, Hot Shot, and he slipped while you were going over a jump. You fell off, hit the jump, and he landed on top of you."

"Was I killed?"

"No, stupid, but you were hurt. Now, we can't have you with a broken arm, because that takes too long to heal. I've got it. You got a real bad concussion, and you lost your memory."

"Sure, and I wandered around the woods in a daze for two months and just happened to end up in Vermont, working for you," Kerry finished for her sarcastically. "Come on, Holly, we've got to do better than this. Liz won't believe a word of it. Why don't we just tell her I had a bad fall, lost my nerve, and quit riding. She'll believe that. It's happened before, you know."

"That sounds okay," Holly said hopefully. "Besides, she'll be so thrilled to have you on the team she probably won't pay much attention to the story."

"Okay, that's it, then," Kerry said with relief.

Kerry felt as if a ton of bricks had been lifted from her shoulders. As much as riding Magician the night before had helped, talking to Holly and sharing her secret had helped even more. With Holly's friendship to support her, Kerry knew that she could now look forward to getting back into the swing of riding again.

"I think I'll go down to the stables this afternoon," Kerry said. "Want to come with me?"

Holly shook her head. "No, I don't think so. The sun feels too good. I'm going to lie here all afternoon and turn into a broiled lobster. But you go ahead, and don't forget to give Magician his carrot. There's some in the refrigerator."

After Kerry had made a quick lunch and made sure that Holly had everything she needed, she changed into a pair of jeans and sneakers and set off for the stables. How marvelous it felt to be looking forward to going there instead of dreading it and pretending to be scared. She didn't think anyone else would be there. Liz had taken the younger kids to the horse show, along with Susan and Robin to help her out. She seriously doubted that either Whitney or Monica would be around.

Magician and the other horses who were left at the stables had been turned out to graze in the large paddock behind the barn. There was a small clump of trees in the far corner, and all the horses were sheltered underneath it, lazily swishing at the flies with their long tails.

Kerry climbed onto the fence and straddled it, the same way she used to at Sandpiper Stables. As she sat there, gazing at the horses, she remembered the carrots in her pocket. She called out to Magician, and he looked up at her. "Come on, boy, I've got something for you," she called out in a coaxing voice. He stood still, his ears pricked forward. "Come on, Magician. Here's your carrot." Kerry held out her hand with the promised treat.

"I don't blame him for not coming anywhere near you," an icy voice said right behind her. "Why would he trust *you*? You're a horse killer."

Kerry froze in a panic. In a split second her mind shot backward in time, and she could hear Mrs. Mueller's voice hurling accusations at her.

"I'm not, I'm not," she heard herself saying hoarsely to the unseen person behind her. Gradually her tumbling thoughts subsided, and she looked around, half expecting that no one was there. Maybe she'd imagined everything.

But she hadn't. Standing not ten feet away from her was the last person she wanted to see.

"What are *you* doing here?" she gasped out.

"I might say the same for you," Whitney drawled ominously, her pale eyes never leaving Kerry for a moment. "But, of course, we all know what a sneak and a liar you are, don't we, Kerry Logan?"

"What do you mean?" Kerry asked slowly, her mind working furiously. How on earth had Whitney found out? *What* had she found out?

"Maybe I ought to get my mother to call Sandpiper Stables and get the whole story," Whitney said in a threatening voice.

"How did you find out?" Kerry choked out.

"I went to the barn last night," Whitney replied. "I'd left my radio in the tackroom. Holly wasn't the *only* person who saw you ride." She paused, her mouth twisting into a horrible smile. "I must say, you really had us all fooled with your stupid play-acting. But after what you told Holly, I'm not surprised you had to keep it quiet."

"It was an awful accident," Kerry said desperately as all her old guilt came crashing back.

"No, it wasn't," Whitney snapped. "You admitted you were in a hurry. You really did leave that stall door without latching it properly, and yet you knew that horse was good at escaping from his stall. I bet you did it on purpose."

"No!" Kerry yelled. "That's not the way it was. You're twisting it." Her anger started to rise, and she took a step toward Whitney.

"I wonder what Liz Chapman would do if she found out she had a liar and a horse killer living in her house," Whitney said in a low voice. "You know, my mother really wouldn't approve of that. She's very fussy about the kind of people who are hired to do the work around here." She paused and looked down her nose at Kerry. "And that's all you are, you know. Just the hired help, even if you do pretend to be Holly's friend."

Kerry's jumbled mind suddenly thought about how worried Liz was about having her contract renewed by the Homeowners' Association. If Mrs. Myers found out about her past, she'd force Liz to fire her. Or worse, she'd fire Liz! That was something Kerry didn't want to have on her conscience. It was overloaded enough as it was.

As calmly as she could, she faced the girl in front of her. "All right, Whitney. What do you want?"

Whitney smiled. "I knew you'd catch on," she said smoothly. "I'm sure you don't want Liz to lose her precious job, or for you to have to leave yours. It's really quite simple. All you have to do is give up your secret riding on Magician and promise that neither you nor Holly will ever tell Liz that you can ride." Her nasty smile widened as she continued to stare at Kerry's hostile face. "See, I told you it was simple, didn't I?"

"Why are you doing this to me?" Kerry managed to croak out. Her throat had started to close up, and she began to feel dizzy.

Whitney's smile faded. "I don't want you on our riding team. And I know that once Liz sees you ride, she'll want you on the team. There's no place for you at Timber Ridge, Kerry Logan. You're not one of us, and the sooner you get that through your head, the better."

"That's *blackmail*!" Kerry shouted at her.

Whitney shrugged. "Call it whatever you like," she said in a carefully controlled voice. "But it's not as bad as what you did. You killed a horse." With that, she turned around and walked swiftly away, leaving Kerry in a trembling rage.

Numbly Kerry pulled her hands out of her pockets and stared at the carrot she was still holding. With tears in her eyes she looked at the horses again. Somehow, as if sensing her distress, Magician left the group and trotted up to the fence. He stuck his nose between the rails and nuzzled her hand, gently taking his carrot.

"I'm so miserable," Kerry wailed, wishing he could answer her and make her feel better. She climbed the fence and leaned against his soft, warm neck, her hands entwined in his mane. She wished over and over again that she hadn't chosen last night to ride. It was all such a mess, and for a moment she didn't know what to do.

Magician nudged her gently, as if he knew she was feeling rotten. Kerry hugged him fiercely, then let him go. "It's no use," she said to him in a strangled voice. "I've got to get back to the house and tell Holly what's happened. There's no way we can talk to Liz now."

"I can't believe she'd really go through with it," Holly said after Kerry had finished telling her about her meeting with Whitney.

"I can," Kerry muttered miserably. "She means what she says, Holly. If we tell Liz, and I start riding, Whitney will get her mother to cause the biggest fuss you've ever seen."

Holly nodded her head. "You're right, but I can hardly believe it. What on earth are we going to do now?"

"Nothing," Kerry said in a flat voice. "Absolutely nothing. Things will just go on the way they always have. You'll ride Hobo, I'll jump and hide in the corner whenever a horse comes near me, and Whitney will keep on making fun of me. Just like always."

"I *hate* her," Holly said vehemently. "I wish there was *something* we could do."

"There isn't."

Chapter Seven

The expression on Liz Chapman's face when she walked through the front door left no doubt how the trip to the horse show had gone.

"That bad, huh, Mom?" Holly asked.

"Even worse," Liz said with a sigh as she dropped her canvas bag onto the floor and pulled off her riding boots. She looked at Holly and gave her a lopsided grin. "And please, will you promise to shoot me if I ever tell you I'm going to put Laura Gardener and Marcia Myers in another equitation class together. Okay?"

"Sure, Mom," Holly agreed with a laugh. "But why?"

"Because they almost tried to kill each other, that's why. And after it was over, I almost killed Mrs. Myers." Liz groaned and sank wearily into a chair. "You know, there's got to be a better way to make a living. There has to be."

"Come on, Mom," Holly said gently. "You know you love it. Look, I'll make you a sandwich. Then you can tell us what's got you so steamed up." She went into the kitchen and added another sandwich to the list. "Mom's had a lousy day," she muttered to Kerry quietly. "She sounds as if she's at the end of her rope, and she's really worried about the show next week."

"Holly, tell me more about the competition," Kerry said curiously. "Is it a three-day event?"

"Sort of," Holly replied. "It's an annual thing, put on by the Hampshire County Hunt Club. They have dressage, cross-country, and jumping, and they also judge the teams on their stable management."

"How many teams enter?"

"I think there were nine last year," Holly told her.

"Did Timber Ridge compete?"

Holly nodded. "They came in fifth place. Mom was delighted, but Mrs. Myers wasn't. She yelled and screamed at Whitney for not winning the individual medal. You should have heard her! I thought Whitney was going to die from embarrassment."

Kerry shuddered. Mrs. Myers sounded like the worst sort of horse show mother—the kind who was always criticizing her kids and getting mad if they didn't win. "Why is Mrs. Myers so all fired up about Timber Ridge winning this event?" she asked as she tore off a piece of lettuce to add to Liz's sandwich.

"It'll give her something to show off about, for one thing," Holly answered. "And I have a sneaking suspicion that she's pretty much promised the Homeowners' Association they'll have a winning team."

"Talk about counting your chickens before they're hatched!" Kerry muttered with a grin.

"Yeah, and if the team doesn't win, Mrs. Myers is going to look like a fool. You see, she doesn't know the first thing about horses, except what Whitney tells her. So, naturally, Whitney has her mother convinced that she'll win the medal and the team will win the challenge cup. I guess it's her only defense."

"What do you mean?"

"I think Whitney's mother only loves her when she's winning blue ribbons," Holly replied quietly.

"Ugh, how awful!"

A worried look passed across Holly's face. "All I know is, Mom's really uptight. She's just got to get that team into shape by next Friday."

"Holly, something's been sort of bothering me," Kerry said carefully. "I mean, if Liz doesn't like it here, why don't you move away? She's a really good instructor, and I bet she could get another job anywhere."

Holly's eyes misted over. "It's because of me," she said quietly. "My accident cost Mom almost everything she had. The insurance wasn't nearly enough, and there's not much left. Plus, this house already has a pool, and Mom wants me to swim."

Kerry muttered a quiet "Oh." She didn't know what else to say.

Early the next morning Holly was awakened by the telephone. She let it ring, figuring Kerry or Liz would pick it up. Then she remembered she was in the house alone. Kerry had gone shopping, and Liz was already at the barn. Half-asleep, she reached for the phone. "Hello," she mumbled sleepily.

It was Susan Armstrong, and she sounded awful.

"Holly, is Liz there?" Sue's voice sounded hoarse and very faint.

"No, she's at the barn. What's the matter? You sound sick." Holly paused, a feeling of dread rushing through her. "Sue, tell me you're not sick. Please!"

"Holly, you're not gonna believe this, but I've got the chicken pox."

"What?" Holly exploded into the phone. "Come on, stop kidding around. Kids your age don't get chicken pox."

"Oh, yes, they do," Sue answered quietly. "My twin nephews are covered in spots, and guess who they gave it to? Mom's just called the doctor, and I've been ordered to stay in bed."

"For how long?"

"At least a week. Maybe longer. The doctor told Mom that chicken pox is more serious the older you are."

"Sue, that's awful!" Holly cried. "And the championships are next weekend." She almost dropped the phone as she realized what Sue was trying to tell her.

"I can't ride," Sue said miserably. "I'm sorry, but there's nothing I can do. Look, Mom's yelling at me. I've got to get back to bed. Tell your mother for me, okay? I'll try and call you later."

Still stunned by the news, Holly dropped the phone. With Sue Armstrong sick, the team was finished. They had to have four riders, and there wasn't anyone else at the barn good enough to take her place.

61

Or was there? Holly started to grin. Maybe there *was* something she could do, but first she had to get hold of her mother. Quickly she grabbed the phone again and dialed the barn's number.

"Mom," she said breathlessly when her mother answered. "Can you come home? Something's happened, and I've got to talk to you right away."

"What's the matter?" Liz sounded worried. "Are you okay?"

"I'm fine, but Sue isn't. She just called. She's got the chicken pox, and she won't be able to ride next weekend."

Liz groaned loudly. "Oh, no," she cried. "Now what am I going to do?"

"That's what I want to talk to you about," Holly replied impatiently. "But not on the phone."

"You're not going to suggest that I let you ride, are you, Holly? Because, if you are, I'm not in the mood for a stupid joke."

"No, Mom. I'm not, but please hurry. I've got a lot to tell you."

Holly waited anxiously by the kitchen door. In less than five minutes she saw her mother running down the path.

"I don't know what's on your mind, Holly," Liz said breathlessly as she ran into the house, "but before I do anything else, I've got to call Mrs. Myers and tell her I'm canceling the team from that competition. There's no way we can compete without Sue."

"Mom, don't," Holly said urgently. "Not till you hear what I've got to tell you."

"Unless you're going to pull another rider out of

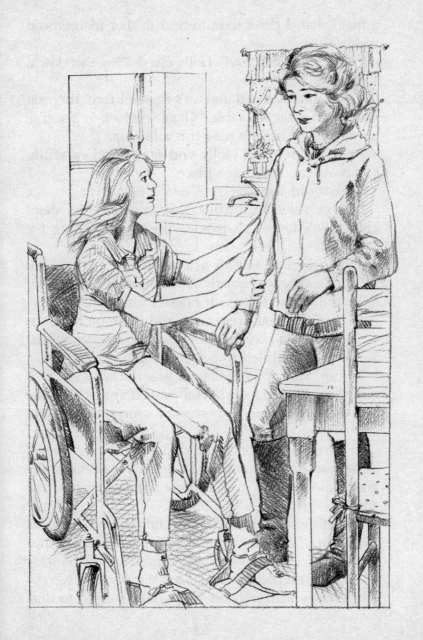

a magic hat, I don't want to hear it," her mother said testily.

"That's just it. I *can!*" Holly cried. "Now, sit down. Please."

Liz stared at her daughter's flushed face, then sat down at the kitchen table. "Okay, you look as if you're about to boil over. What's this all about?"

"Kerry can ride," Holly said slowly and carefully. "And *she* can take Sue's place."

"What did you say?"

"Kerry rides beautifully. I've seen her. On Magician. She's better than Sue. She's been riding for years."

Liz looked at her in astonishment. "Kerry can ride?" she repeated quietly. "I don't understand, Holly. Why didn't she tell us? It doesn't make any sense."

Liz's expression grew more and more incredulous as Holly slowly and carefully told her everything that Kerry had confided to her that night in the barn.

"Mom, you don't believe it was Kerry's fault that the horse died, do you?" Holly asked anxiously. "She blames herself, but I know she's wrong. She's got to be."

"I agree with you," Liz said quickly. "Kerry doesn't strike me as irresponsible. I'll bet you anything there was someone else in that horse's stall *after* her that night."

"That's what I think," Holly said. "But how can we find out? We don't even know where Sandpiper Stables is."

Liz frowned and reached for the phone. "Kerry's Aunt Molly will probably know." She started to dial.

Holly held her breath. She hoped Kerry wouldn't be too mad at her for spilling the beans. But this was an emergency, and if there was some way for Kerry to ride and save the team, Holly knew she'd do it.

"Did she know the number?" Holly asked when Liz had finished talking to Kerry's aunt.

Liz nodded and started to dial the phone again.

Holly let out a sigh of relief. "Now, if only Kerry's mistaken about that stall door," she said quietly.

Chapter Eight

Holly listened to her mother's part of the conversation and tried to guess what was being said on the other end of the phone. But it was impossible. Liz just frowned a few times, nodded her head, and said brief sentences like, "Are you sure?" and "How terrible for you." Just when Holly thought she was going to burst wide open with curiosity, her mother's face broke into a broad smile.

"Thank you for telling me all this, Mrs. Mueller. Good-by."

"Mom!" Holly shrieked as she pushed a kitchen chair out of her way and tried to maneuver her wheelchair closer to the telephone. "What did she say? Was it Kerry's fault?"

Her mother collapsed into a chair and, for a second or two, said nothing.

"Come on, Mom, you're driving me nuts!"

"It wasn't her fault, Holly. You were right, thank

goodness," Liz replied happily. She reached out and grabbed Holly's hand and gave it a loving squeeze.

"So what really happened, then?" Holly asked impatiently.

Liz took a deep breath. "Black Magic did get out of his stall and into the feed room, just as Kerry said. When he colicked and died the next morning, Mrs. Mueller was frantic. She blamed Kerry. She feels really awful about that now, Holly. She asked me to apologize to Kerry for her."

"But if it wasn't Kerry's fault, why didn't Mrs. Mueller call her and tell her? How could she have let her go on thinking she'd killed that horse?" Holly asked.

"Because by the time the real cause of this whole mess finally surfaced, Kerry had come here. Mrs. Mueller didn't know how to contact her, and her father had already left for the Middle East."

"So tell me what she said!" Holly insisted.

"Well, after Mrs. Mueller had finally calmed down, she decided to have the vet do an autopsy on the horse. She'd begun to be suspicious about the colic. She said it was because the horse hadn't been acting quite normal for several weeks."

"So what did the vet find?"

"It wasn't colic that killed Black Magic. It was a tumor in his intestines," Liz said quietly.

"I see," Holly said thoughtfully. "But he did get out of his stall and pig out on the sweet feed. That can't have been very good for him."

Liz shook her head. "No, it wasn't, but he was like a walking time bomb, Mrs. Mueller said. He could have died at any minute."

"But, Mom, I still don't think this will make Kerry feel much better. I mean, she feels really rotten about forgetting to latch his door properly."

"There's more," her mother said mysteriously as she got up and opened the refrigerator door. "I'm thirsty. Do you want some iced tea or something?"

Holly shook her head. "Don't stop, Mom. The suspense is killing me."

Liz poured herself a glass of iced tea and sat down again. "After Mrs. Mueller told everyone at the stables that Black Magic's death was because of a tumor, she had a visit from a very upset riding student—a girl named Janet. Apparently Janet had been at the stables *after* Kerry that evening, and she had gone into Black Magic's stall to give him some more water. She'd noticed that his bucket was almost empty, and she filled it."

"So then *she* was the one who didn't do the door up properly," Holly said slowly. "Why didn't she own up to it instead of letting Kerry take all the blame? The rotten little sneak!"

"She was scared. And when Kerry went away, Janet thought she'd just keep her mouth shut."

"I'm not surprised," Holly said grimly.

"But when Mrs. Mueller got the results of the autopsy and told everyone about the tumor, Janet figured that she really wasn't to blame after all. She decided to own up to the truth about the stall door."

"Mom," Holly said excitedly, "you know what this means now, don't you?"

"Yes, we can get Kerry to take Sue's place on the

68

team. Thank goodness we found out the truth. Now maybe we have a chance of winning. But"—she paused briefly—"I only hope you're not exaggerating about Kerry and the way she rode Magician. You're not, are you, Holly?"

"No," Holly replied vehemently. "Just wait till you see her, Mom. She's terrific."

"Well, let's hope she gets back soon so we can tell her the good news. If she's going to take Sue's place, we haven't got a minute to lose!"

Holly sat quietly in a corner of the kitchen, watching Kerry's face as Liz told her the good news. When her mother had finally finished recounting everything that Mrs. Mueller had told her, Kerry started to cry.

"Don't, Kerry, it's all over. Don't cry," Liz said soothingly.

"I'm sorry," Kerry sniffed. "I'm crying because I'm happy, that's all. Are you sure it's true? I mean, I'm not dreaming all this, am I?"

Liz laughed. "No, of course you're not. Mrs. Mueller is really sorry, Kerry. She hopes you'll forgive her for not believing in you. She also told me what a good rider you are. Holly says the same thing. So why don't we go down to the stables, and you can impress me as well."

"What are you going to tell Whitney and her mother?" Holly asked suddenly.

"I figured that the truth would probably be best," Liz said with a smile. "I'll have a quiet word with Whitney first and set her straight, then just tell Mrs.

Myers that we have a replacement for Sue. Now let's go!"

Thirty minutes later Liz stood in the middle of the outside riding ring and watched as Kerry rode Magician over a course of practice jumps. "You were absolutely right," she said happily to Holly, who was sitting close beside her, enjoying the riding performance almost as much as if it were she who was in the saddle instead of her best friend.

"Do you think we've got a chance now?" Holly asked anxiously.

"Much better than before," her mother answered quickly as Kerry took Magician expertly over the double oxer right in front of them. "She's got a natural talent, Holly. She's easily as good as you were."

"I know," Holly replied happily.

"Liz, can I talk to you?" Whitney's shrill voice suddenly came floating across the ring.

Liz turned around abruptly and saw that Whitney and Monica were leaning on the rails, watching the horse and rider closely. "In a minute!" she yelled back.

"Good luck, Mom," Holly said under her breath. She wished she could listen in on the conversation, but she knew her mother wanted to handle it alone. She'd have given almost anything to be able to see Whitney's face when her mother told her that Kerry was going to be a part of the riding team.

Kerry had also noticed Whitney's sudden arrival at the riding ring, and for a moment her confidence slipped a couple of notches. As she cantered around slowly, she hoped that Holly had been wrong. They

71

only had four days to get ready for the competition, and if Whitney somehow managed to pull an unexpected trick on them, it would be all over.

She slowed Magician down to a walk and glanced toward the rails. Liz was deep in conversation with Whitney, and from the look on the girl's face, Kerry knew they weren't out of trouble yet.

Chapter Nine

Kerry had never worked so hard in her life! But she happily endured the agony of stiff muscles as Liz patiently coached her and Magician.

There was so much to learn, and so little time. Dressage was the easiest, but only because Magician was so well trained. Kerry memorized the test and practiced riding it in the outside ring under Liz's critical eye. For hours at a time she walked, trotted, and cantered around the ring, being careful not to cut her corners, and trying to remember which carefully memorized movement came next. Whenever Kerry had tried to explain dressage to someone who didn't ride, she always told them it was like the compulsory figures competition in ice-skating.

Magician excelled on the cross-country course. His powerful legs ate up the distance, and he soared over the jumps like a big black bird. At first he was so eager to run that Kerry had a hard time holding him back. All he wanted to do was race.

Liz set up a course of jumps similar to the ones at the last Hampshire Classic, and Kerry joined the rest of the riding team as they practiced for the last time. She tried as best she could to keep out of Whitney's way, but it wasn't easy.

"Magician will make mincemeat out of those jumps!" Holly said confidently. And she was right. One by one, Magician leaped over the brightly colored obstacles, and all Kerry had to do was steer him in the right direction.

"Okay, kids, that's enough!" Liz announced after they'd all jumped the course three times. "We're as ready as we'll ever be."

The day before the show dawned with gray, overcast skies. But Kerry's spirits were anything but gray when she arrived at the barn. Everything was going along just great, and so far, Whitney hadn't done anything to mess things up. Maybe she was safe.

While Holly took Magician's saddle and bridle apart for its last cleaning, Kerry got busy grooming her horse. He'd rolled in some dirt, and his coat was filthy, but she didn't care. Grooming him was part of the fun, and she started by brushing him vigorously with a stiff dandy brush.

Magician curled his lip up when she brushed the mud out of his withers. He had a ticklish spot there, and he was doing his version of a horsy giggle! Then Kerry switched to the softer body brush and, with wide, sweeping strokes, ran the brush over his fine black coat until it gleamed.

"Shall I braid his mane?" she asked Holly when

74

she'd finished brushing him.

"Of course," Holly said. "He wants to look pretty."

Kerry found a box of small elastic bands in the tackroom and went to work on his mane. First she separated his mane into small bunches and secured them with an elastic. Then she tightly braided the first hunk near his ears, folded the braid underneath, and wrapped it carefully with the small black elastic band. By the time she finished, Magician had fifteen tiny braids all down the crest of his neck. He looked gorgeous, and he knew it! Then she braided his forelock, and he kept pushing her gently with his nose.

"Now he looks like a real dressage horse!" Holly agreed.

Kerry picked up one of the reins Holly had been cleaning. It felt as soft as butter. She knew she was going to look terrific when she finally got into the ring. Holly had cleaned her tack, she'd groomed Magician to perfection, and Aunt Molly was altering one of Liz's hunt jackets for her to wear. She was all ready to go.

Her good mood vanished the minute Whitney and Monica came into the barn. It was the sneaky expression on Whitney's face that did it.

"Liz, I've got to talk to you!" Whitney announced in a loud voice. She glanced at Kerry. "Too bad," she said. "All that hard work for nothing."

"What are you talking about?" Holly snapped. She wheeled herself up the aisle toward her mother's office. "Mom, where are you?"

Kerry felt as if her heart had just dropped into the

pit of her stomach. Just when she was feeling confident that nothing could go wrong, somehow it had. Whitney's sneering face told her that.

"What is it, Whitney?" Liz said from inside her office. "I'm on the phone."

"I'll wait," Whitney replied smoothly. She leaned against the doorway and waved a small book in front of Kerry and Holly.

"Okay," Liz said when she finished her phone conversation. "What do you want, Whitney?"

Whitney grinned at Monica as she handed Liz the book. "I think you'd better read page twenty-one," she said ominously.

"What's this?" Liz looked at the small book and frowned.

"The Homeowners' Association Rules and Bylaws," Whitney replied. She looked at Kerry and shook her head. "Kerry can't ride after all."

"Mom, where does it say that?" Holly demanded angrily.

Liz sighed, and her face looked grim as she handed the book back to Whitney. "I'm afraid Whitney's right," she said. "There's a rule that says any person representing Timber Ridge Manor in a sporting event must be a resident."

"But, Mom, Kerry *is* a resident!" Holly protested. "She lives with us."

"She only *works* here," Whitney snapped, her pale blue eyes flashing with pleasure as she stared at everyone. "And she's not eligible to ride in the horse show."

"Boy, are you stupid, Whitney," Holly said with a

sly grin. "If Kerry doesn't ride, the team can't either. You've got to have four riders."

Kerry held her breath. Holly was right. Maybe it wasn't all over.

"Wrong, Holly Chapman!" Whitney yelled. "A team can have three riders if they want. Only the top three scores from each team count for the prize anyway."

Holly turned accusingly toward her mother. "Mom, did you know about that?"

Liz nodded, her face looking grim. "Yes, we need four riders. You never know when something's going to go wrong."

"Nothing will go wrong!" Whitney cried triumphantly. "We don't need Kerry Logan at all."

Kerry felt tears pricking at the corners of her eyes. Angrily she wiped her face. There was no way she'd give Whitney the satisfaction of seeing her cry.

"Poor Kerry," Whitney said suddenly. "Why don't we hire her as our groom? I mean, if she can't ride in the competition, it seems a shame not to let her come along anyway. She might be quite useful. I'm sure she'd love to help us out. Wouldn't you, Kerry?"

Kerry turned away without saying anything. She was too choked up with disappointment and anger. Instead, she untied Magician from the cross-ties and led him back into his stall. She put her arms around his neck and tried to feel better. But even he couldn't comfort her. Whitney had ruined everything, just as Kerry knew she would.

Dimly she heard Liz telling Whitney and Monica to groom their horses and clean their tack. The show would go on without her; but with only three riders, the Timber Ridge team didn't stand a chance of winning.

She was still hugging Magician when Holly came into the stall a few minutes later. "Don't give up yet, Kerry."

"Huh?" Kerry pulled her tear-streaked face away from the comfort of Magician's warm neck. "What are you talking about? You heard what Whitney said. I can't ride, and that's that!"

"Sshhh!" Holly warned. She glanced back over her shoulder. Whitney and Monica were directly across the aisle in Astronaut's stall. "I don't want them to hear."

"Hear what?"

"Robin Lovell's mother is on the Homeowners' Committee. She's going to call an emergency meeting tonight. She's going to get them to change the rules! Mom told Robin what happened, and she called her mother right away."

"Can they do that?" Kerry asked anxiously, her hopes starting to rise again.

"Mrs. Lovell thinks so," Holly whispered. "But we won't know anything till later tonight. She's promised to call Mom by ten o'clock."

Kerry tried to cheer up, but it was no use. Deep down she was scared to death that Whitney and Mrs. Myers were going to win.

Chapter Ten

The telephone rang at ten-fifteen. Kerry and Holly both looked anxiously toward Liz as she picked up the receiver.

"Oh, hello, Mrs. Russell," Liz said, trying not to sound too disappointed.

Kerry sunk back onto the couch. It wasn't the call they'd been waiting for. She looked at the clock, wondering again how long the committee was going to take.

"That was your aunt," Liz said to Kerry a few minutes later. "She's bringing the jacket by tonight. It's all finished, so let's hope you get a chance to wear it."

Kerry forced herself to smile, but as the minutes ticked slowly by, she began to feel even more miserable. After all the work she'd done in the past few days, she couldn't bear to think that it could all come to nothing.

"What's taking them so long?" Holly asked, yawning. "I don't think I can stay awake any longer."

"Go to bed," Liz said. "I'll stay up. If it's good news, I'll wake you up."

Just as Kerry got up to help Holly into her room, the phone rang again. She held her breath as Liz reached out for the receiver.

"Zero hour," Holly muttered ominously.

Both girls watched with bated breath as Liz nodded a couple of times. Then she broke into a delighted smile. "Thanks, Mrs. Lovell. Yes, you've made my day."

"Whoopee!" Holly yelled at the top of her voice. She reached up and grabbed Kerry, pulling her into the wheelchair with her.

"We're on, girls," Liz said happily above the shrieks and yells coming from Holly's wheelchair. "Now, let's go to bed and get some sleep. We've got a lot to do in the next three days."

They were on the road just before six the next morning, still very tired, but excited about the days ahead. Liz drove the stable's large horse van with its four precious animals safely secured in their traveling stalls. Holly, Kerry, and Robin were all squeezed into the front seat beside her. Holly's chair was with the saddles, bridles, and tack trunks in the back, along with several bales of hay, sacks of grain, and endless amounts of assorted horse equipment.

Whitney Myers's face had been pinched with anger earlier that morning as they loaded the horses into the van. She and Monica had disappeared soon after.

They were driving to the show grounds with Mrs. Myers.

"The ground's still pretty wet and slippery," Liz warned as they pulled into the long driveway that led to the show grounds, "but it should be dry by tomorrow for the cross-country."

Kerry looked out of the window. Ahead, she could see several large white tents, with brightly colored flags fluttering in the gentle breeze. They drove past two riding rings. One was full of jumps, painted in a wide variety of colors and decorated with pots of red, pink, and white flowers. The other ring, off to their right, was bordered by a low white fence and marked off with large capital letters that identified it as the dressage arena.

Several other riding teams had already arrived by the time Liz parked the Timber Ridge van in the large field that was serving as the competitors' parking lot.

"That's the Larchwood team," Holly said, pointing toward a huge red and black horse van.

Kerry read the words painted on its side: "Larchwood Equestrian Club, Larchwood, Vermont." She turned to Holly. "They won last year, didn't they?"

"Yes, and the year before that too. They're awfully good. And if they win for the third time in a row, they get to keep the challenge cup."

Liz stopped the motor and looked at her eager young companions. "Okay, girls, this is it," she said softly. "Let's get to work. Holly, you take care of this." She handed her a pile of papers. "Check which stable numbers we're in while we unload the horses."

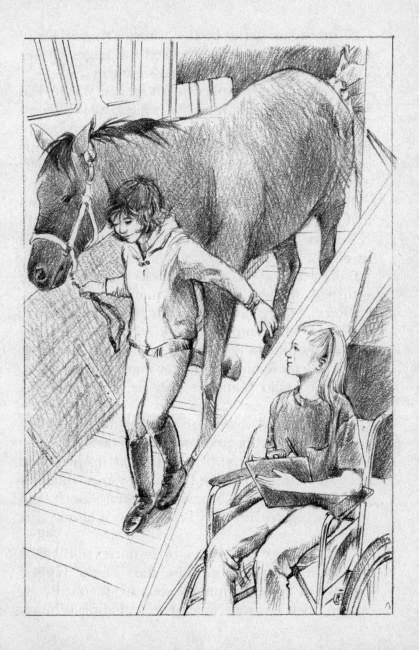

"I guess you get to be the 'director,' huh?" Kerry teased as Holly quickly checked the pages on her knee, looking for their stable assignments.

"You bet," Holly replied in an excited voice. "You know, this is the first time I've come to a horse event with Mom in two years. I never wanted to before because it hurt too much. Now with you riding in my place, and because I'm *sort of* riding again, I'm really excited. Aren't you?"

Kerry nodded, and then she walked up the ramp and started to unload the four horses. With Robin's help, they got all four animals settled into their stalls in only a few minutes. Liz went off to check last-minute details at the show secretary's tent. When she returned, she had four riders' numbers with her.

"Kerry, you're riding last, I'm afraid," she said as she handed her number thirty-two. "Apparently, they put all the numbers in a box and pulled them out like a lottery. Robin, you've got number four, Monica's fifteen, and Whitney's right before Kerry. She's number thirty-one."

She explained that there were eight teams competing, each with a full complement of four riders. "Kerry, why don't you help Robin get ready for the dressage test; she'll be in the ring by nine-thirty or so. Monica will probably ride just before lunch, and you and Whitney at about four o'clock this afternoon."

The next two hours flew by as horses and riders prepared themselves for the start of the biggest equestrian event for junior riders in the county. By nine o'clock everyone was there, including Whitney and Monica, who'd arrived with Mrs. Myers in her large silver Mercedes.

"When will they start judging the stable management part of this?" Kerry asked Holly as they sat by the dressage ring, waiting for Robin's turn to ride.

"They've already begun," Holly said, pointing toward the stable area. Kerry looked up and saw a man and a woman, holding clipboards, walking slowly up and down in front of the horse stalls, looking inside as they went.

"Thank goodness I cleaned Magician's stall a few minutes ago," Kerry muttered, then she turned her attention back to the riding ring. The crowd was applauding loudly as a boy riding a dark chestnut horse left the ring.

"He's one of the Larchwood riders," Holly informed her. "Good, isn't he?"

Kerry nodded. "Do they score this like a normal competition?" she asked as a girl on a large gray horse trotted in, ready to begin her test.

"No. They have their own peculiar system. Each rider starts with a hundred points," Holly explained. "Then points are taken away every time someone makes a mistake. You know, like if a horse refuses a fence, or messes up on the dressage test. Mom says they're pretty strict about the stable management, too. They'll probably deduct points if they find more than five flies in Magician's stall at once!"

Kerry giggled, and tried to stay calm.

"Robin's next," Holly whispered anxiously. "Keep your fingers crossed for her."

Tally Ho looked beautiful and relaxed as his rider

calmly trotted and cantered him around the ring, following the precise movements of the dressage test. The crowd clapped with enthusiasm as they left the ring. Kerry hoped she and Magician would do as well when it came to their turn.

Several more horses and riders competed, and Kerry's turn was getting closer. She started to pace back and forth, reciting the required moves under her breath. She was concentrating so hard, she didn't notice Whitney and Monica staring at her.

"That won't help you win the gold medal," Whitney said sarcastically. She nudged Monica, and they both giggled. "You might as well forget about it, Kerry, because I'm going to win, and you can't stop me."

Kerry didn't answer. As Whitney and Monica ran off, she had the horrible feeling that Whitney wasn't through with her yet.

Chapter Eleven

Kerry sat quietly on Magician's back as she watched Whitney riding in the dressage arena. As the girl on the big bay horse trotted and cantered around, Kerry's thoughts were firmly fixed on one thing. She had to clear her head of everything except the dressage test that she had so carefully memorized.

As the spectators applauded number thirty-one's almost perfect performance, Kerry picked up her reins and started trotting her horse in a small circle. In just a few more minutes it would be her turn.

Whitney rode past her, a triumphant smile on her face, and then the judge's bell rang, signaling the next, and last, rider into the ring.

Kerry's heart started to beat faster, and all of a sudden her mind went completely blank. She'd forgotten the test! In a daze she steered Magician toward the entrance gate and trotted down the centerline, hoping her memory would return.

Did she turn right or left at the end of the arena? She couldn't remember! She halted briefly and nodded her head, saluting the judges. Then, miraculously, her mind cleared, and without realizing it, she started her test.

Magician's stride was even and balanced. Kerry completed her circle, then swung into the second one, making a perfect figure eight. At marker K in the corner she slowed to a walk, rounded the narrow end of the arena, and walked across its diagonal. At the judges' stand she squeezed Magician gently with her legs and urged him into a slow trot, sitting firmly in the saddle as they went from one end of the arena to the other. So far, so good. Then she urged him into a canter. Her body rocked gently back and forth as the beautiful black horse cantered down the well-worn path toward the judges' stand. Don't look at them, Kerry cautioned herself as she swept past. Concentrate!

She repeated the pattern again, cantering in another circle, then she trotted Magician diagonally across the ring, making him extend his stride. His powerful shoulder muscles rippled beneath her, and the bright sunlight danced off his gleaming black coat.

At the far end of the ring, Kerry turned Magician toward the judges for the last time. She halted squarely in front of them, nodded briefly, and left the ring at a relaxed walk. The first part was over, and when she heard the audience's enthusiastic applause, she knew she'd done well.

"That was a good ride," Liz said as she patted

Magician's neck. "A very good ride. I don't think you racked up too many penalty points for that one."

"Marvelous," Holly said in an exaggerated drawl. "I knew you could do it once you stopped worrying and let Magician take you around the course. I bet he had it memorized better than you!"

Kerry gasped. Holly was right. He *did* have the dressage test memorized, because at the end of the arena, when she hadn't been sure whether to turn left or right, the horse had steered her in the right direction after all. "Good boy," she said fondly, and leaned forward to rub his ears.

"Come on, Kerry," Liz said urgently. "Get him into his stall and clean him up. They'll be looking at the horses very closely tonight. I'm going to check on the points so far," she said. "And, Robin, I want you in bed early. You'll be riding at nine tomorrow morning, and you need as much sleep as you can get." She left the group and went to the secretary's tent, hoping that the results of the dressage test were posted.

They were. But only the teams' overall standing. Larchwood was predictably in the lead with a total of 320 points, Sunshine Stables had 312, and Timber Ridge was in third place, with 301.

"What about the individual points?" Whitney asked crossly.

"We won't know those till Sunday morning," Liz informed her sternly. And then her voice softened a little. "Whitney, please try and forget about the individual medal. We're all here as a team, and we need to stick together. Okay?"

Whitney tossed her head arrogantly. "Whatever you

say," she muttered sarcastically, then walked stiffly away to join her mother and Monica. They were getting ready to leave the show grounds and go to their hotel for the night.

"Well, Whitney hasn't tried anything so far," Holly said to Kerry as they got ready for bed. Mrs. Lovell had generously loaned the riding team her family's motor home.

"Hmmmm," Kerry murmured sleepily.

"I'm so excited about tomorrow, Kerry. Aren't you?" Holly pulled the patchwork quilt over her shoulders and turned to face Kerry in the opposite bunk. "It's almost as much fun as if I were riding!"

"Stop talking, girls!" Liz commanded from the double bed she was sharing with Robin. "You can talk all you want in the morning."

As Kerry drifted off to sleep, she couldn't stop thinking about the cross-country course. Three and a half miles of trails and jumps through the woods. Jumps with frightening-sounding names like Tiger's Trap and Water Hazard!

Chapter Twelve

"Ugh, this bed feels like a plank of wood!" Kerry mumbled when she woke up the next morning. Her back was stiff, and she had a crick in her neck.

"I know," Holly agreed, "but it's better than sleeping in the horse van. Come on, let's get going."

They arrived at the start of the cross-country course just as the first rider galloped through the starting gate. "I want to check the course map," Kerry said.

"There's at least ten jumps," Holly said as she studied the chart carefully. "Magician's been on lots of courses like this before, so you shouldn't have any trouble."

"How about the Water Hazard?" Kerry asked, remembering how Black Magic had always hated water. He'd dumped her off once in the middle of a stream, and she'd had to walk all the way back to the barn, soaking wet.

"No problem," Holly assured her with a laugh. "Magician's middle name is Fish. He loves water, but you'll have to make sure he doesn't swim in it. Just keep him going and don't let him stop. If he does, and starts to paw at the water, belt him one with your crop. Otherwise he'll lie down and try to roll."

For the next few hours Kerry practiced staying calm. Every time she started to worry about the cross-country course, she recited nursery rhymes or tried to remember the names of all the horses she'd ever ridden. When that didn't help, she carefully undid Magician's braids and brushed his mane.

Robin Lovell completed the course with only a few faults, and she rode back excitedly to warn Kerry about what was waiting for her.

"The worst hazard is all the spectators," Robin said as she got off her horse. "There's a huge crowd at the water, and almost as many by the Tiger's Trap. Just watch out for the kids, that's all. Tally Ho almost took one out as we got near the jump. Thank goodness the kid's mother pulled her out of the way in time, or we'd have had a minced three-year-old splattered all over the course!"

Kerry and Holly laughed. Kerry actually started looking forward to her ride. One by one, the riders took their turns. Monica, looking nervous and frightened, galloped off on Silver Dust, and Kerry hoped she would make it around without an accident.

"I hope you've memorized the course properly," Whitney said as she sat on Astronaut, waiting her turn. "It gets very tricky toward the end."

Kerry nodded without saying anything, wondering what Whitney was up to now. But she knew there was no way the girl could harm her once she was on the course. Whitney would be too busy riding Astronaut to have any time to mess things up.

Liz gave Whitney some last-minute instructions, then she was off.

"Good luck!" Kerry yelled generously. She wanted Whitney to do well for the sake of the team. She could see how pleased Liz was with the way things were going, and unless something went terribly wrong, they had a good chance of placing in the top three.

"Okay, Kerry, you're next," Liz called out.

Kerry lifted her leg forward in the saddle and tightened her girth. Then she adjusted the chin-strap on her crash helmet and pulled on her leather riding gloves.

"Just let Magician do all the work," Holly said urgently as the starter signaled for the last rider to get ready. "And don't forget what I said about the water. I wasn't kidding! You'll end up swimming if you don't keep him moving."

Kerry nodded, then she was off. For the first few hundred yards, she had to fight with Magician to keep him from galloping too fast. He was excited and wanted to run. But Kerry knew from experience that she had to make him go slower in the beginning so he'd have enough speed and energy to finish the course where the jumps were the toughest.

As she jumped the low rustic cross-rail, Kerry tried to clear her mind so she could concentrate on the course. It was marked with red and white signs. Small, colored triangles set on four-foot posts. Keep

the white on the left, and the red on the right, she said to herself over and over again.

Gradually she let Magician lengthen his stride, and they cleared the next two fences as if they were nothing more than a couple of shoe boxes. Horse and rider galloped down the hill, Kerry's slight body poised over the horse's center of gravity.

"This is fun!" she cried as Magician gathered himself up and flew over the log pile.

Kerry didn't hear the applause behind her. She was conscious only of the steady, thudding rhythm of Magician beneath her. "Tiger's Trap comes next," she muttered. Magician twitched his ears as if he understood her.

Instinctively, Kerry tightened her grip on his body. She shortened her reins, and when they were only a few strides away from the infamous Tiger's Trap, it happened!

A sudden flash of color—a flag, or a piece of cloth, waved right under Magician's nose. Magician shied violently sideways, and Kerry suddenly found herself hanging around his neck, almost out of the saddle.

"Don't panic," she muttered. "I won't fall off!" She pulled herself back into the saddle and took control. Magician was trying to turn away from the jump. Kerry knew they'd get penalty points if he did. "Easy boy," she said as calmly as she could, as she pulled him back on course. Then she looked around to see what had frightened him.

Just as she was about to urge him toward the jump, she caught sight of Marcia Myers, Whitney's ten-year-old sister, scowling at her from the edge of the crowd. She was holding something bright orange. Kerry looked closer. It was a windbreaker, or a sweatshirt, and that was what had scared her horse only moments before!

In a flash Kerry knew that Whitney hadn't given up. Grim determination settled over her, and she dug her heels into Magician's sides. He only had time to take three strides before the jump, and the Tiger's Trap was one of the toughest! It had several rows of large logs, with enough space between them so that both horse and rider could clearly see what was on the other side—a dark, scary ditch! It was the sight of that ditch that made many horses refuse the jump.

"Please don't refuse!" Kerry whispered into Magician's mane. She gripped tightly with her knees and closed her eyes as he took off.

Thud! They landed safely on the other side. Kerry heaved a sigh of relief. Surely Whitney didn't have any more little sisters handy to do her dirty work for her. Or did she? What would the next two miles of the course bring her way?

The course got narrower, and Kerry slowed down to a canter as she followed the twisting path between huge pines and cedars. Then the path widened, and Kerry felt Magician's impatience. He wanted to run!

"Go on, boy!" Kerry shouted. There were no spectators to hear her, and she reveled in the feeling of power that riding this magnificent horse produced. She leaned into his flying mane and felt it whipping across her face.

Suddenly they came out of the trees into strong

light. For a moment or two Kerry was blinded. Her memory of the next obstacle blurred, and she took it badly. Magician lost his stride and was awkwardly positioned for the next jump.

"Sorry, boy," Kerry gasped out as she struggled to keep her balance. Magician corrected himself and leaped over the wide ditch. Then, as if he knew the course by heart, he turned a sharp corner and went straight over a tree trunk between the colored marker flags.

"You're fantastic!" Kerry cried. "You could do this without me!"

Ahead, the course opened up into a large field, and she knew that the water was next on the list. Kerry slowed Magician down so that she could check her watch. They were making excellent time, in spite of the near miss in front of the Tiger's Trap.

"Okay, boy, slow down," she warned as they galloped toward the river. "This isn't a race. We'll only get penalty points if we come in too late."

Crowds of people had gathered at the Water Hazard; and when she saw it, Kerry knew why. It was the biggest she'd ever seen. And it looked deep enough to drown in!

Magician's ears pricked forward as they approached the shimmering water. It was part of a slow-moving river, and the horse and rider had to scramble down the short, steep bank, jump into the water, go downstream for about fifty yards, and then jump a set of low poles in the shallow edge by the other side before climbing back out again.

"Okay, Magician. Let's go," Kerry whispered to her

horse. And then she remembered Holly's warning. "And don't you dare swim!" she added as he eagerly plunged into the water, making an enormous splash. He stopped and started to paw violently at the water with his left foreleg.

The crowd roared in appreciation. Kerry knew they were probably all hoping that rider number thirty-two would take an unexpected swim. She brought her crop firmly down on Magician's rump and kicked him with her legs. He lurched forward, the water swirling around his belly. Kerry kept him moving.

When they reached the shallow water, Magician popped easily over the jump and scrambled his way up the steep bank on the other side of the river. Kerry hung on to his mane and almost slipped backward, out of her saddle. "Good boy!" she whispered loudly.

Applause and shouts of "Well done!" sounded in her ears as she left the crowd behind and plunged into the woods. But where were the familiar red and white markers?

Kerry slowed down and looked around anxiously. How could she have gone wrong? Reluctantly, she pulled Magician back to a slow trot and stood high in her stirrups, hoping to catch sight of the next course marker. There had to be one around somewhere.

Slowly and carefully she made her way between the trees and bushes, the path getting narrower and narrower. "Oh, Magician, we're lost!" Kerry wailed miserably. "I don't know where the trail's gone!"

Losing precious minutes, Kerry frantically looked for a red or white triangle. Magician seemed to sense her anxiety. He picked his way carefully between the trees as Kerry searched for a course marker. Then, she saw something odd. It was a broken stick, standing upright in the ground, just ahead of her. It looked suspiciously like one of the posts that the course markers were attached to.

Kerry trotted up and took a closer look. It *was* a course marker stick, and she'd almost missed it. But where was the red or white triangle that was supposed to be on top?

"Let's go, Magician!" she said breathlessly, and the horse lunged forward, cantering as fast as he could on the narrow trail. He seemed to know that they had to make up for lost time.

Whitney again! She must have broken the markers off when she rode by, knowing Kerry was right behind her.

Magician's coat was soaking wet with sweat, and Kerry wasn't much better off. Nervously she wiped her hand across her forehead and forced herself to concentrate on the rest of the course. When the woods gave way to the last piece of open land before the finish, she leaned forward and urged her horse into a flat-out gallop. He flew effortlessly over the next two jumps, and finally, ahead of her, she could see the gentle uphill climb to the finish line and the last jump in the course.

"We're gonna make it!" she yelled as she pushed Magician even faster. He surged forward and raced as if his life depended on it.

Holly and Liz both stared at the big time clock on

the show secretary's mobile van. Kerry only had two minutes to get back before her allotted time ran out.

"Mom, what do you think has happened to her?" Holly asked anxiously, her eyes never leaving the clock.

"She'll make it, don't worry," Liz assured her, but her voice didn't sound very convincing. Whitney had already completed her ride, but there was still no sign of the last rider.

"She'll get penalty points if she doesn't show up soon," Holly moaned.

"There she is!" Liz cried out suddenly.

"Where?" Holly and Robin said together.

"Just coming out of the woods. Oh, come on, Kerry. You can make it!" Liz shouted.

The crowd seemed to realize the tenseness of the situation. Anxious eyes veered back and forth between the big white time clock and the approaching horse and rider.

"One more fence," Holly said, holding her breath.

Kerry and Magician approached the last obstacle, a long, low picnic table, complete with red and white checkered tablecloth that flapped gently in the breeze.

Kerry felt Magician's stride falter as they got closer. "Don't refuse, please!" she implored. "It won't hurt you!" She knew how much horses hated things that flapped and decided this jump was far worse than any of the others.

She kicked him once and willed him forward with all the strength she had left in her tired body. Magician summoned one last ounce of energy, and without a moment's hesitation he lifted himself up and soared magnificently over the top.

"Yippee!" Kerry shrieked as they thundered home between the finish posts to loud clapping and cheering.

Exhausted and trembling, Kerry slipped off Magician's back. When her feet hit the ground, she almost crumpled up. Both she and her horse were breathing heavily. Magician was covered in sweat. Kerry flung her arms around his neck and buried her face in his damp mane. "We did it," she said quietly. "We did it!"

Liz rushed up to her. "What happened out there?" she asked breathlessly. Before Kerry had a chance to answer, Liz threw a blanket over Magician's back so he wouldn't get a chill. "You'd better walk him around," she said.

"I got kind of lost," Kerry said shortly. "Did I get any time faults?"

"No, you were back with ten seconds to spare," Liz informed her happily. "Did you have any refusals?"

Kerry shook her head.

"That means you went clear," Liz said cheerfully. "Well done. We've probably moved up a notch now. Whitney says she went round clear, and Robin and Monica had one refusal each."

Half in a daze, Kerry continued to walk Magician around, cooling him off before she put him back in his stall. As her temper subsided, she wondered whether she ought to confide in Holly about what Whitney had tried to do. She couldn't make up her mind. So far, none of Whitney's sly tricks had worked. And they only had one more event ahead of them.

What could the girl possibly do to her in the jumping ring in full view of everyone?

and led Magician into the stable and gasped in shock. When she'd left it just over an hour ago to ride the cross-country course, it had been perfectly clean. She remembered picking up all traces of

Chapter Thirteen

"Kerry, what happened to your stall? It's a mess!" Holly shrieked.

Kerry led Magician into the stable and gasped in shock. When she'd left it just over an hour ago to ride the cross-country course, it had been perfectly clean. She remembered picking up all traces of manure and putting down a fresh layer of shavings.

"She finally got me!" Kerry snapped angrily, looking at the piles of fresh manure that littered the floor. Magician's water bucket was hanging lopsided on its chain, and bits of leftover hay were strewn around the dirty bedding.

"What are you talking about?" Holly demanded. Then she paused and said, "Oh, no! Not Whitney!"

Kerry nodded curtly. Then she told Holly about Whitney's other attempts at sabotage. "I'd better clean this up before the judges come around again," she muttered miserably. She took Magician back outside and tied him up. Then she found a pitchfork and a manure basket and went to work.

"I'm going to tell Mom," Holly announced in an angry voice.

"No, please don't," Kerry said quickly. Deftly, she scooped up a pile of soiled bedding and tossed it into the already overflowing basket. "She'll only get worried, and she's got enough on her mind as it is. Don't say anything. I'll handle this myself."

"How come we've only got 276 points?" Robin exclaimed early the next morning. Liz had just returned from the secretary's tent with the news that Timber Ridge was in second place, one point ahead of Tall Pine Farm, and twenty-two points behind the leaders, Larchwood Equestrian Club.

"Don't complain, Robin," Liz said as she handed out a bag of fresh doughnuts and cartons of orange juice. "We've moved up a notch, and I think that's great. Don't you?"

Kerry knew that the judges had seen Magician's stall, and they'd deducted five penalty points. Quickly she finished getting dressed and dashed outside to get ready for the jumping. Timber Ridge still had a chance!

Robin managed the jumping course with only ten penalty points, but Monica's horse refused three times, and they were eliminated from the competition.

"That means there's just the three of you now," Liz said with a worried frown as Kerry tacked up her horse. It was thirty minutes before she was due in the ring, but she wanted to have plenty of time to warm him up over the practice fences before they had to jump.

"Do we have a chance, Liz?" she asked anxiously as her instructor gave her a leg up. She landed gently on Magician's back.

"Yes, I really think we do," Liz replied thoughtfully. She checked her notebook, made some rapid calculations, and then said, "Larchwood has one more rider to jump, and right now they've got 275 points. We have 266, and Tall Pine is all through riding, and they've only got 225."

Kerry quickly sorted out the numbers in her head. "If Whitney and I get clear rounds, and Larchwood's last rider gets more than nine faults, we'll win?"

"Yes," Liz said with a smile. "Look, she's going in the ring now. Just keep your fingers crossed."

Kerry walked slowly around on Magician and tried to watch the Larchwood rider jump the course. She waved to her aunt Molly who had arrived to watch the jumping, and then began concentrating on working Magician over the practice fences. The last Larchwood rider had got ten penalty points. It was all up to her and Whitney!

As she watched Whitney and Astronaut clear one fence after another, she wondered what the individual riders' points were. There was no way of knowing because the show committee hadn't posted any individual scores.

The crowd went wild, clapping and cheering, as Whitney and Astronaut cantered out of the ring. They'd had a clear round, and Kerry knew from the look on Whitney's face that she was confident of winning the individual medal.

Let her, Kerry thought to herself as she gathered up her reins and trotted Magician into the jumping ring. All I care about is getting round clean so that we can win the team prize.

The starter's whistle blew, and she was off. Kerry forgot about everything else except the course in front of her, and her nervousness vanished as she approached the first fence.

Magician cleared the cross-rail with hardly any effort at all and cantered steadily toward the brush jump. Up and over he went, his feet grazing the leafy branches. Kerry checked him slightly and turned toward the parallel bars.

"Easy, fella," she whispered urgently. Magician's ears were pricked forward and he wanted to race! "One, two, and three," Kerry counted as Magician gathered himself up for the takeoff. As his powerful body leaped into the air, she felt herself slipping sideways.

"Oh, no!" she cried, snatching a handful of mane. And just in time. Her right stirrup flew away from the saddle and banged noisily against the jump post as she landed on the other side.

"Aaaggghhh!" The crowd erupted in an agonized gasp as they watched her struggle to stay in the saddle. Their cries of alarm changed to cheers when Kerry righted herself and swung her left stirrup in front of her saddle.

"Atta girl!" someone shouted. "You can do it!"

Kerry's pulse was racing, and her hands trembled as she tightened her hold on Magician's reins. "Okay,

boy, take it easy now," she said grimly. Jumping without any stirrups at all was far safer than jumping with only one, but she didn't relish completing the course with only her knees to keep her in the saddle.

She turned Magician to face the double oxer. "Don't jump too big!" she cautioned him as he cantered toward the red and white poles. I'm not going to fall off! I *won't* fall off! she repeated silently to herself.

Magician lengthened his stride just in front of the jump. He flew over it as Kerry crouched against his flying mane.

The audience clapped loudly, but she hardly heard them. Her legs were aching, and she longed for the relief that stirrups would bring. Cutting diagonally across the ring, she faced her horse at the five-bar gate and the barrels. The gate was a solid three-and-a-half feet high, and Kerry held her breath. Could she jump it without her stirrups?

"Go, go, go!" she whispered urgently to Magician. He flicked his ears back and forth, and soared over the gate. Three strides, and then he jumped the barrels.

Crack!

One of his hind feet had touched the pole on top of the barrel jump. Kerry held her breath, waiting for the clunk that would tell her it had fallen down. But nothing happened except the roar of an excited crowd. She was clear . . . so far.

Two more jumps, and it would be all over! Carefully she angled Magician around so that he could take a long, fast run at the in and out. He had to be able to get in two very long strides between the two fences in order to get over them successfully.

"Go for it!" Kerry could feel his muscles straining as he charged toward the jump. But her cries quickly turned to horror.

"Oh, no! It's too soon . . ." Her voice was choked off as Magician leaped forward. He should have taken another stride. They'd never make it!

Kerry threw herself forward, praying she'd stay in the saddle. The horse soared over the jump, took two strides, and then cleared the second one.

"You wonderful horse!" she cried with relief when they landed safely on the other side. "One more jump, boy, and we're home free!"

The audience was perfectly quiet as horse and rider thundered toward the last jump on the course. To Kerry it looked like the worst she'd ever seen. Her leg muscles were screaming for mercy, and she wished she could just fly off Magician's back and put an end to her pain!

The red brick wall stood at almost four feet. It was decorated with pots of pink and white geraniums.

"Don't stop and eat them!" she warned Magician as they drew closer to the jump. He flicked his ears and strode eagerly forward as if he could sense that the end was in sight.

Kerry tried to hold him back, but she checked him too late. He put in one last, short stride before the takeoff. He was too close to the jump. They were going to knock it down!

If only she had her stirrups! Desperately, Kerry wound her fingers through Magician's mane as he shot straight up in the air, his nose almost grazing the jump. We'll never make it! she thought. We're going to land right on top of it!

With an extraordinary effort, Magician bunched his legs underneath his belly, and Kerry could feel him straining with effort as they sailed over the top.

Thud!

They landed safely on the other side, and Kerry could hardly believe she was still in the saddle. Scenery and spectators rushed by like speeded-up film as she rode across the finish line. Flashes of color, snatches of noise.

The crowd went wild, cheering the horse and rider that had just had a clear round. In a daze Kerry realized that Timber Ridge had just won the Hampshire County Classic.

Chapter Fourteen

"We won! We won!" Holly yelled at the top of her voice as Kerry and Magician cantered out of the ring.

Smiling faces and helpful arms crowded around Kerry as she slithered off Magician's back. As soon as her feet hit the ground, she collapsed. She couldn't even feel her legs! "I went clear, didn't I?" she said hoarsely, as if she couldn't quite believe it.

"Yes, you did!" Liz cried. "And without stirrups, too!"

"You did it! We've won!" Holly yelled again.

Magician lowered his head and nudged Kerry. She was still sitting on the ground, half in a daze. She grinned and circled his nose with her arms, kissing him gently on his soft, warm muzzle. "You wonderful horse, I *love* you!" she said happily. Magician snorted softly and pushed her over.

"What happened to your stirrup, Kerry?" Liz reached down and helped Kerry to her feet. "I don't know how you managed to get round that course without them. That was some performance you put on out there!"

Kerry winced as she put weight on her feet. "I guess it wasn't on properly." She leaned against her saddle and looked at the remaining stirrup leather. It was kind of close to the end of the metal bar it was attached to, and she gave it a sharp tug. It came off in her hands. "I should have checked them before I went in the ring."

One of the ring stewards ran up and returned the flyaway stirrup. "Thanks," Kerry muttered as she took it from him. She slipped both stirrup leathers back onto her saddle, making sure they were securely in position.

"Stirrups don't usually go flying off into outer space without some help," Holly whispered quietly. She glanced toward her mother, but Liz was busy talking to Robin Lovell. She hadn't heard her.

Kerry frowned at her, knowing she and Holly were thinking along the same lines. But she had no way of knowing whether this latest mishap was Whitney's fault or not. "Forget it," she said under her breath. "It was just an accident."

"I *bet*!" Holly snorted sarcastically.

"Don't say anything," Kerry warned. She didn't want Holly to make an issue out of it. The competition was over, and there was nothing else Whitney could do to hurt her.

Holly shrugged, then grinned. "Okay, sure. We've won the cup, and that's all that matters right now."

"Not so fast, kids," Liz interrupted. "We'd better

not count our chickens before they're hatched!"

"What are you talking about, Mom?" Holly said. "We won, didn't we?"

"I don't know," Liz replied, studying her notes closely. "The judges have to add up the three best individual scores from each team. And don't forget, Monica was disqualified. I don't know how that will affect us."

"Did I win the medal?" Whitney interrupted rudely.

"Oh, shut up!" Holly snapped angrily. "Can't you think about anyone else except yourself and that stupid gold medal?"

"My, my, aren't we nasty today," Whitney sneered.

"Ladies and gentlemen," the loudspeaker boomed loudly above them. Instantly an expectant hush settled over the crowd of spectators and competitors. "Before we announce the team results of the Hampshire County Classic, we'd like to bring you up to date on the individual riding results. A very unusual thing has happened here today. It seems as if we have not one, but *two* talented young riders who are tied for first place."

Whitney's blush faded instantly; and as Kerry shot her a quick glance, she noticed that Whitney was clenching her fists.

"Will riders thirty-one and thirty-two please come to the judges' stand?"

Whitney's face broke into a delighted smile, which then faded almost as fast as it had arrived. She looked at Kerry, a mixture of astonishment and hatred on her face.

"Go on, you dummy," Holly squealed with excitement, and she pushed herself up to Kerry and shoved her forward.

Kerry almost fell over. "What did you do that for?"

"Boy, Kerry Logan, you're deaf as well as dumb!" Holly shrieked. "It's *you*! You're number thirty-two, aren't you?"

With a gulp of astonishment, Kerry looked at her friend and started to laugh.

"Hurry up," Holly said, "or else they'll think you don't want it. Go on."

"I'll go with you," Liz said proudly. "After all, it's not every day a riding instructor gets *two* individual gold medal winners in the same show." She looped her arm through Kerry's and dragged her into the ring at a run.

"Congratulations, ladies," the judge said to the two young riders standing in front of him. Then he looked at Liz. "Are you their instructor, ma'am?"

"Yes," she answered proudly.

"I'm afraid we've got a bit of a problem," he said gravely, looking at the medal in his hands. "We weren't expecting a tie. So if you don't have any objections, I'd like your two young riders to share this." He handed the medal to Liz.

This is where we bury the hatchet, Kerry thought to herself, and without a moment's hesitation she grabbed Whitney's hand. "We've *both* won, Whitney. Let's share the medal." She smiled hopefully. If only Whitney would agree, it might help to wipe out all the tension that existed between them.

Whitney's eyes grew cold, and she jerked her hand away. For an instant she stared at Kerry, no hint of

a smile on her face. "I don't want to share the medal," she said scornfully. "Can't we have a ride-off?"

The judge looked surprised. He coughed twice, checked his watch, and whispered to the man standing next to him. "Um, I suppose you can. We've got time."

"Whitney, the horses are exhausted!" Liz protested.

"Astronaut's fine," Whitney snapped. Then she stared at the judge. "Well, what do we have to do?"

"Go back to the collecting ring, and I'll make an announcement in a few minutes," he said with a sigh.

Kerry's heart sank. She didn't want to ride again. Her legs couldn't stand the punishment. "Come on, Whitney, why don't we just toss for it?" she said as a last resort.

"We'll ride!" Whitney turned around abruptly and walked stiffly back across the ring.

Liz put her arm around Kerry's shoulders and squeezed her. "Thanks for trying to patch things up with Whitney. I know she's not easy to work with."

They walked slowly back toward Holly, who was waiting anxiously inside the collecting ring. "Well, what happened?" she asked as soon as they reached her.

"Whitney and I are going to ride for the medal," Kerry said quietly. "Poor Magician. He's done enough." She patted his neck and adjusted the blanket that Robin had thrown over him.

Just then the loudspeaker crackled into life again. "Will both finalists please lead their horses up to the judge."

"Good luck!" Holly cried as Kerry whipped Magician's blanket off. She dumped it on the back of Holly's chair and walked back into the ring.

Liz, Robin, and Aunt Molly gathered around Holly's chair, watching the activity in the center of the ring. When it became apparent what the judge wanted them to do, Liz cried out in astonishment. "Oh, good grief! They're making them switch horses!"

Holly laughed. "This ought to be fun! Whitney's never ridden Magician before. I bet she falls off. Oh, I can't wait."

Whitney's eyes opened wide with horror as the judge told them what to do. "I want to ride my *own* horse," she protested angrily.

"I'm afraid this is what we've decided," he replied patiently. "You could always toss for the medal, you know."

Whitney hesitated for a few seconds. If she won the toss, she'd get the medal and she wouldn't have to ride Magician. But if she lost . . . Whitney shuddered. Her mother would be furious if she backed down and accepted the toss of a coin.

"No, I'll ride," she said grimly. She reached out and snatched at Magician's reins. "And I'll ride first."

"Go easy on his mouth," Kerry said quietly as they switched horses. She hated the thought of the heavy-handed rider hurting Magician's soft, responsive mouth.

"I know how to ride," Whitney snapped. She mounted Magician awkwardly and jerked on the reins as she landed hard in the saddle. The black horse

118

flicked his ears back and forth, and Kerry saw the whites of his eyes. That was a bad sign. Magician was obviously unhappy about the change of riders.

While the ring stewards rearranged the jumps, Kerry stood quietly beside Astronaut and watched Whitney as she tried to warm up on Magician. The horse looked miserable, and Kerry couldn't bear to watch. His nose was in the air, trying to evade the bit in his mouth, while Whitney kept tugging on the reins.

Desperately, Kerry battled with her feelings. She really wanted to win the gold medal, but not at Magician's expense. If only they didn't have to switch horses. She glanced at Whitney again. The ring steward was explaining the new course of jumps to her, and all of a sudden Kerry knew what she had to do. Thoughts of Liz losing her job, and Mrs. Myers' angry face shot through her mind, reinforcing the decision she'd just made.

She led Astronaut over to the judge. "I've changed my mind," she said quietly. "I'm withdrawing from the competition."

The judge looked at her in astonishment. "Why?"

"I, er . . . I hurt my leg when my stirrup flew away," Kerry lied, saying the first thing that popped into her mind. "It's hurting, and I don't think I can ride."

The judge slowly nodded his head, and Kerry limped back to the collecting ring, pretending to favor her right leg. Just as she reached Holly and Liz, the announcer informed an astonished audience that the winner of the individual gold medal was Whitney Myers, from Timber Ridge Stables.

"Kerry, *why*?" Holly asked. "You would have beaten her!"

"I know, but I couldn't bear to watch her ride Magician. Did you see the way she was pulling on his mouth?"

Holly nodded grimly and reached out for Kerry's hand. "Thanks for saving my horse from being mauled around."

Liz, who had overheard the conversation, put her arm around Kerry's shoulders. "That was a very unselfish thing you just did."

Kerry gritted her teeth as a triumphant Whitney rode out of the ring to a scattered round of applause. Giving up that gold medal had hurt. She really wanted to beat Whitney, especially after all the awful things she had done. But then she started to think about Liz's job. Maybe Mrs. Myers wouldn't be so anxious to cancel her contract now that her daughter had the precious gold medal in her hot little hands.

"Here's your horse!" Whitney said scornfully. She jumped off Magician's back, clutching her medal. "I beat you, Kerry Logan. Fair and square. You chickened out!"

"No, I didn't," Kerry retorted quietly so that Liz and Holly couldn't hear what she was saying. "I'd have beaten you, and I will, the next time." She gently took Magician's reins and threw Whitney a challenging look.

"Ha! There won't be a *next* time. You'll never ride for the team again."

Before Kerry had a chance to reply, Mrs. Myers ran up, breathless with excitement. She brushed right past Kerry without even noticing her. "Well done, darling," she gushed as she put her arm around Whitney's shoulders. "I knew you could do it. And we can display your beautiful new medal in the trophy case with all the others you've won. I'm so proud of you, and I can't wait to show . . ."

Whitney shot Kerry a scornful look as her mother led her away, still talking a mile a minute. Kerry almost felt sorry for her.

"And now, ladies and gentlemen," the loudspeaker boomed above them, "we have the results of the team competition. . . ."

Holly tightened her grip on Kerry's hand.

"The winner of the Hampshire County Challenge Cup is the team from Timber Ridge Stables, and in second place . . ."

Kerry didn't hear the rest of the announcement because her excited teammates were all yelling and laughing at once. Liz had tears streaming down her face, and Holly looked as if she was about to burst with excitement!

Kerry felt a warm glow inside, and her smile grew wider. They'd done it! The team had won!

As Liz hugged her daughter, Kerry put her arms around Magician's neck. "Thank you," she whispered softly into his silky mane. "You're the best horse in the whole world!"

"You can say that again!"

Kerry turned around and saw Holly smiling at her,

a wistful expression on her face. An image of Holly, riding Magician, wild and free as the wind, suddenly flew into her mind. "You'll ride him again, Holly. The way you *used* to. I just know you will."

And she had a special, magical feeling that she was right.